THE CASE OF THE
AUTUMN ROSE

THE DAVIS DETECTIVE MYSTERIES

THE CASE OF THE
AUTUMN ROSE

RICK ACKER

Kregel
Publications

The Case of the Autumn Rose

© 2003 by Rick Acker

Published by Kregel Publications, a division of Kregel, Inc., P.O. Box 2607, Grand Rapids, MI 49501.

The persons and events portrayed in this work are the creations of the author, and any resemblance to persons living or dead is purely coincidental.

Cover illustration: Kevin Ingram

Library of Congress Cataloging-in-Publication Data
Acker, Rick.
The case of the autumn rose / by Rick Acker.
    p. cm.
   [1. Pearls—Fiction. 2. Fathers and daughters—Fiction.
3. Vietnam—History—1975—Fiction. 4. Brothers and
sisters—Fiction. 5. Mystery and detective stories.] I. Title.
PZ7 .A1813 Cas 2003
[Fic]—dc21   2002152252

ISBN 0-8254-2004-0

Printed in the United States of America

1 2 3 4 5 / 07 06 05 04 03

*Again, the kingdom of heaven is like a
merchant seeking beautiful pearls, who,
when he had found one pearl of great
price, went and sold all that he had
and bought it.*

—Matthew 13:45–46 NKJV

THE CASE OF THE
AUTUMN ROSE

TOO MANY WAYS TO DIE

April 12, 1975, 12:22 A.M.: Saigon, South Vietnam

The rising moon saved Pierre LeGrand. For a few seconds its quiet white light shone through a break in the black midnight clouds and in through his bedroom window, silhouetting a man standing on the roof of the building across the street. He had an AK-47 assault rifle slung across his back, and he was watching Pierre's window with binoculars. Then the clouds closed and the moonlight vanished, again hiding the watcher in darkness.

Pierre froze for a moment as he lay in bed, thinking furiously. How many of them would there be? Where? How much time did he have? He had feared this moment would come, but he had no idea it would come so soon. He would have to find a way to accelerate all his plans. Somehow.

He slipped quietly out of bed. "Where are you going?" his wife asked. Her voice wasn't at all sleepy.

So you know about this, he said to himself. He was angry and hurt, but not surprised. "I'm just going to get a glass of water. Would you like anything?"

"No thanks," she said, faking a yawn. "Just hurry back. You know I can't sleep when you're out of bed."

He went into the bathroom, closed the door, and turned on the faucet. He let the water run as he climbed on the toilet seat and slid back a tile in the ceiling. He pulled out a black sweatshirt and sweatpants and quickly put them on. Next came special shoes with soft, silent rubber soles. Then a charcoal stick to rub over his face until it was covered in dull black. He grabbed a coil of mountain climbing rope, his gun, and a velvet pouch on a string that contained something small and round. He tied the string around his neck and carefully tucked the pouch into his shirt. What he was carrying was very valuable, and he didn't want to lose it.

Then he reached up into the ceiling, grabbed a beam, pulled himself up through the hole, and slipped the tile back into place. He crawled along the beams in the narrow space between the ceiling and the roof for about twenty feet until he reached a trapdoor in the roof. Workers once used it to repair wiring and plumbing in the crawlspace, but it had been forgotten for years and now Pierre was the only one who knew about it. Or so he hoped.

He opened the trapdoor and lifted himself onto the roof. He lay flat for a moment, listening. There was no sound except the night breeze. He got up carefully and looked around the flat asphalt roof. A North Vietnamese soldier crouched at the roof's edge, looking down over the LeGrands' apartment. This soldier could see all the windows that were out of sight of the man with the binoculars, but his back was to the trapdoor. He hadn't seen Pierre, but he was right next to the fire escape, which Pierre needed to use to get off the roof. Pierre had to get past him quickly. And quietly.

Pierre crept soundlessly behind the soldier, but his luck gave out: Just then a car honked somewhere behind him. The soldier came from the farm country of the North where cars were rare, and the horn startled him. He turned toward the noise and saw Pierre standing just three feet away. The soldier's reflexes were fast, and he jerked his gun up and fired a quick burst at Pierre.

But Pierre's reflexes were faster. As soon as the soldier saw him, he dropped down flat and the bullets shot harmlessly over his head. Pierre swung his leg around and kicked the soldier's feet out from under him. The soldier fell and dropped his gun. Pierre hit him hard in the back of the head to knock him out. The man collapsed heavily and lay still.

Pierre heard voices shouting and the sound of a gun firing from the rooftop across the street. So much for his hopes of escaping unnoticed. Pierre grabbed the soldier's rifle and fired two short bursts in the direction of the man with binoculars. That should make them think twice about coming over to get him.

He dropped the gun and slid down the handrails of the fire escape. He heard more shots as he hit the ground. Little splashes of dirt a few feet away showed where the bullets struck. He dove behind a hedgerow and ran in a half-crouch between the building wall and the bushes. Then he ducked down a dark alley between two three-story buildings. At the other end of the alley, a drainpipe came down the side of one building, right where the alley opened into a wide street.

Pierre stopped and climbed up the drainpipe, as fast and silent as a cat. He crouched behind the low edge wall on the roof of the building. Running footsteps entered the alley below. They ran past the pipe, then stopped. He could hear low voices talking in tense tones. Several long seconds passed in silence. Then he heard the sound of someone taking hold of the drainpipe and starting to climb up. He took out his gun and aimed it at the spot where the pipe came up to the roof.

A truck drove by and a man's voice shouted from the street. Bursts of machine-gun fire echoed through the night as the truck stopped. A grenade exploded in the alley and the gunfire got closer. Pierre heard more shouting and the top of the drainpipe shook. A second later, he heard a thump from the alley below and several sets of feet running away.

Pierre risked a quick peek over the edge of the roof. His gamble had paid off: The street at the end of the alley was a favorite route for South Vietnamese troops retreating from the battles to the north. A truckload of them had spotted the North Vietnamese chasing Pierre and had attacked, driving his pursuers away. *It's a good thing they don't know I'm up here,* he thought as he ran lightly along the rooftop and used his rope to let himself down the opposite side. The South Vietnamese generals weren't his friends either. At least not anymore.

Now came the hard part. He had to get across the city and to the harbor unseen. He would have to escape the watchful eyes of the marines and harbor police (who would be looking for him) and find a boat and make it to the *Tiger's Eye,* a cargo ship that a friend had said could smuggle the two of them out. All of this might have been doable in a few weeks when the North Vietnamese Army was closer (so far the South had hardly slowed them down) and Saigon was full of refugees. Then the city would be chaotic and full of desperate people, and it would be more possible for him to disappear into the crowds. Also, his growing list of enemies would be more worried about getting out of town themselves than keeping him in.

But the North Vietnamese commandos outside his apartment had forced his hand too soon. There were no crowds to hide him now, and no Northern armies marching in to distract his Southern enemies. His plan would have been dangerous enough even if the timing had been right; now it was probably suicidal. But then, so was staying.

His plan might still work, *if* he could make it to the harbor unnoticed, *if* the *Tiger's Eye* had gotten in early (it wasn't supposed to dock until the morning), *if* he could somehow get on board without getting caught, and *if* no one else betrayed him tonight. He shook his head; that was an awful lot of ifs.

He sighed. There were too many ways to die tonight. He wondered briefly which one would find him as he set off across the dark and dangerous city.

CHAPTER 1

A MYSTERIOUS PHONE CALL

June 22, Last Summer, 7:25 P.M.: Glen Ellyn, Illinois

Arthur Davis was just finishing *A Tale of Two Cities,* which was on his summer reading list for English class, when the phone rang. His mother picked it up. "Arthur!" she called upstairs. "It's for the Davis Detective Agency!" Arthur and his sister, Kirstin, had formed the Davis Detective Agency last summer to find lost dogs and catch locker thieves at Glenbard Central High School (where Arthur was a junior and Kirstin was a freshman), but had wound up finding over a million dollars in stolen jewelry and catching a cat burglar who had stumped the police for six months. Since then, business had been booming.

Arthur stood up from his desk and put away his book. His long legs were sore from soccer practice, and it felt good to stretch them. "Thanks, Mom!" he called back. "I'm coming!" He jogged downstairs and took the phone from his mother.

"Hello?" he said into the receiver.

"Hello," said a woman's voice. She had an accent that he could not quite place. "Are you Arthur Davis?"

"Yes."

"Good!" said the mysterious voice. "I want to hire you and your sister to solve a certain small mystery for me. Is she there?"

"Um, just a minute," said Arthur. He put down the phone and went to get Kirstin. He found her lying on her stomach on the floor of her room, her feet up in the air and her shoulder-length blond hair pulled back in a ponytail. She was typing an e-mail on a laptop computer. "Hey, Kirstin," Arthur said.

"Hi, Arthur," she said without turning around. "What's up?"

"There's a lady on the phone who has a new case for us," he said.

"What's it about?" she asked.

"She didn't say yet. C'mon, she's waiting." Arthur jogged down to get the phone in the family room while Kirstin turned on the portable handset. Arthur picked up the receiver and said, "OK, we're both on."

"Good," responded the woman's voice. "As I was saying, I would like to hire the two of you to investigate something for me. There is a horse farm in Downers Grove named the Autumn Rose. I believe your sister rides there. I want to know how it got its name and what they know about a man named Pierre LeGrand."

"Why don't you just call the horse farm and ask?" asked Arthur, a little confused. "I mean, we can always use more customers, but I'm not sure why you're calling us." *And how did you know Kirstin takes riding lessons there?* he added to himself.

"I'm calling you because anyone smart enough to catch that thief is smart enough to investigate a horse farm," said the woman in a slightly nettled voice. "Just find me the information I asked for, and I'll pay you five hundred dollars." Kirstin, who had walked into the family room, looked at her brother. That was a lot of money for such a simple investigation. Why was this woman offering it to them? Kirstin wrote "I don't trust her" on a piece of paper and handed it to Arthur. "Me either," he wrote back.

"I'm sorry, ma'am," said Arthur. "We don't take cases from people we don't know. Good-bye." He was about to hang up the phone when she said, "Wait! You don't know me, but your friend Officer MacGregor knows a Mr. Nguyen who works for me. Ask him."

Arthur and Kirstin looked at each other. If she was up to something shady, would she be telling them to call the police? Maybe they shouldn't turn her down outright. "How can we reach you if we decide to take the job?" asked Kirstin.

There was a brief pause. "You may call me at country code 84, city code 8, 466-5934."

"All right," said Arthur, writing down the number. "By the way, I don't think I caught your name."

"I didn't give it to you," said the voice, "but you may call me Marie."

"Thank you," said Kirstin politely. "We'll be in touch if we can help you."

As soon as they hung up, Kirstin said, "I'll bet that's not her real name."

"I'll bet you're right," said Arthur. "Hey, what's a country code and a city code?"

"I think that's what you use when you're calling a different country," answered Kirstin. "I'll bet I can find something on the Internet." She walked over to the family's desktop computer and sat down.

"Thanks," said Arthur and walked over to watch the monitor over her shoulder.

After five minutes of typing and mouse clicking, he let out

a whistle. "She's calling all the way from Vietnam!" he exclaimed.

"This is all too weird," said Kirstin, shaking her head as she looked at the screen. "Why would some lady from Vietnam care so much about Autumn Rose? And how did she know I ride there?"

"Those are really good questions," said Arthur. He stood up and paced back and forth across the living room, the old polished wood of the floor creaking under his stocking feet as he walked. He was tugging at his lower lip, which he always did when he was thinking hard. The tan skin of his forehead wrinkled under his sandy brown hair. "And I can't think of any good answers. Let's ask Officer MacGregor after the Wednesday evening service tomorrow."

CHAPTER 2

THE DAVIS DETECTIVE AGENCY TAKES THE CASE

Officer Frank MacGregor was a big man with a big voice, so they didn't have any trouble finding him after church the next day. He and Mrs. MacGregor were standing next to the donut table drinking decaffeinated coffee from Styrofoam cups and chatting with friends. He saw them coming and said, "Well, here comes the hero of the soccer game! Nice goal, Arthur! I thought for sure those fullbacks would catch you."

"Thanks, Officer MacGregor," said Arthur.

"*Officer* MacGregor?" The policeman arched his thick black and gray eyebrows. "I should have seen that you two had your business faces on. What can I do for you?"

"Well," said Kirstin, "for starters, this woman from Vietnam said we should ask you about a Mr. Nguyen."

The policeman's face became serious and he nodded. "Yes . . . Yes, I can tell you about Jack Nguyen. Let's sit down. This will take some explaining." They found some chairs and got comfortable. Then Officer MacGregor sat back and started his story. "Jack Nguyen and I were military police together in

Vietnam thirty years ago. He was a great guy. Always had a joke to try on you or a funny story to tell. I was in the army, and he was in the ARVN, the South Vietnamese army. We patrolled Saigon together near the American Embassy."

"Where's Saigon?" asked Kirstin. "I looked at a map of Vietnam, but I don't remember seeing it."

"They call it Ho Chi Minh City now," explained Officer MacGregor, "but back then it was Saigon. The embassy beat was usually a pretty quiet job, but it wasn't on January 31, 1968." He got a faraway look in his eyes as his memory took him back to that day. "We were walking along the street and I was telling Jack a funny story about how bad the Army food was. I remember that because I never got to tell him the funny part. I was interrupted by an explosion ahead of us and the sound of machine-gun fire from the embassy. I heard my sergeant's voice on the radio yelling at us to get to the embassy because it was under attack from the VC." He saw the confused looks on their faces and added, "VC stood for Vietcong, our enemies during the Vietnam War. Sometimes we also called them Charlie.

"Anyway, our soldiers inside the embassy were in trouble, so we ran toward the embassy to help. About halfway there, something hit me in the leg, and I fell down. I heard an AK-47 firing nearby and voices shouting in Vietnamese. I tried to get up, but my left leg wouldn't work. I looked down and saw that I'd been shot. My pants were all covered with blood, and blood was squirting out of a bullet hole in my thigh. I knew that the bullet must have cut an artery and that I'd bleed to death in a few seconds if I couldn't slow down the bleeding. I pulled off my belt to make a tourniquet, but I was getting dizzy from blood loss and had trouble making the tourniquet. Jack bent down to help me, but I told him to go save himself. There were VC all around, and we were out in the open in the middle of the street. They would shoot him any second if he didn't leave.

"I passed out then, so I only know the rest of the story from what people told me later. Jack made the tourniquet for my leg and stopped the bleeding. He only weighed about 130 pounds, while I was over 200, but he managed to pick me up and carry me to the embassy. But by the time he got there, Charlie had taken it over, so Jack had to run for his life again, carrying me the whole time. He got shot then, right here," he pointed to the side of his stomach, "but he didn't leave me. He never left me." He stopped for a moment, took a deep breath, and went on. "Somehow, he managed to get me back to my army base.

"I woke up the next morning in a hospital bed with Jack lying in the bed next to me. The doctor told me what had happened, and at first I didn't believe it. I couldn't believe that a skinny little guy like Jack could carry me all that way, especially after he'd been shot. I also couldn't believe he never left me even though for all he knew I was dead.

"So I turned to him and said, 'Jack, is that true?' He got kind of embarrassed and said, 'Yes, I suppose so.' So I said, 'But how did you do it?' And he pointed to the cross that hung around his neck and said, 'I can do all things through Him who strengthens me.'

"And I knew right then that Jack's God was a real God. I would believe in any God who could make Jack Nguyen so strong and so brave that he would carry me over a mile with bullets buzzing around him like angry hornets and mortar shells exploding everywhere, even though he had a bullet in his own stomach. I *had* to believe in a God like that. How could I not believe in Him after what I had been through? I hadn't been a Christian before, but I asked a nurse for a Bible, and Jack and I read it together and talked about it the whole time until we were well enough to be discharged from the hospital.

"Jack didn't just save my life, he saved my soul." He stopped for a second. "No, that's not quite right, and he'd be the first to say so. *Christ* saved my life and my soul, but He did it through Jack. Without Jack, I would have died on that street." He stopped again and took a deep breath. "So when Jack Nguyen calls, I answer, and I know I can trust him.

"He called me about a week ago and asked if I could help a woman he worked for answer some questions about the Autumn Rose horse farm. I told him I could, but that I knew a young detective named Kirstin Davis who took riding lessons there and that she and her brother might be a better choice. He said that sounded like a good idea and asked me to send him some information about the two of you. I sent him an article about your work on the Lionel Hawkins jewelry case. Did someone call you?"

"Someone did," said Arthur. "I think it was Mr. Nguyen's boss. She sounded pretty suspicious, and we were thinking of turning down the case."

Officer MacGregor looked at Arthur and Kirstin and said, "Well, that's your decision. I won't say anything one way or the other."

The evening air was pleasantly cool as the Davises walked home. The sun had just set, and the crickets and katydids had started to sing. It was a peaceful evening, perfect for settling one's thoughts. Arthur filled his parents in on their talk with Officer MacGregor. After they had walked in silence for about a minute, Arthur said, "So, do we take the case?"

"You're the detectives. What do you think?" asked Mr. Davis.

Kirstin thought for a few seconds more, then shook her head and said, "There's way more going on here than 'Marie' has told us. Until we know more, I say no. How about you?"

"I'm not sure," answered Arthur, "but I'm leaning toward yes. There's a lot we don't know, but we don't really need to know it. All she asked us to do was answer a couple of questions about Autumn Rose. How hard can that be? It sounds like an easy five hundred dollars to me, and I can think of plenty of things to spend that money on."

"*Your share* of the money, you mean," corrected his sister. She kicked a small rock and watched it skitter along the sidewalk before disappearing into the grass of the parkway. "I'm just afraid we'll get sucked into something big that we don't know anything about."

"We'll tell her we won't do any work except this one little job until we know more, OK?" Arthur looked at Kirstin. The light from a streetlight showed the skeptical look on her face, but she nodded reluctantly. "Besides," continued Arthur, "this Mr. Nguyen sounds like a really good Christian, and we know Officer MacGregor is, so even if there is something big we don't know about, I'm sure it's OK."

"No one ever said anything about *'Marie'* being a Christian," objected Kirstin, "and I still don't trust her. How do we know she's not tricking Mr. Nguyen?"

"Good point," said Mrs. Davis. "If you take the case, you'll make sure to keep Officer MacGregor and us in the loop about what you're doing, right?"

"Of course," said Arthur. "And all we really need to know is that we're being offered good money for a simple job. We'll just do the job and take the money, and if she asks us to do anything the least bit suspicious or dangerous, we'll just say no until we have all the facts, OK?"

"It does sound pretty straightforward," commented Mrs. Davis. "If you two are comfortable taking the case, we don't have a problem with you doing it."

"I *guess* I'm comfortable with it," said Kirstin a little uncertainly.

"I *know* I am," said Arthur with a reassuring smile. "This will be a simple little job. Trust me."

CHAPTER 3

A LESSON AT AUTUMN ROSE

Kirstin's next riding lesson was Friday, two days after they had called Marie to tell her they were taking the case. Arthur volunteered to drive Kirstin to the horse farm. That way he could ask questions while Kirstin was riding. In fact, there was a good chance that by the time Kirstin got off her horse, he would have gathered all the information Marie wanted.

Arthur dropped Kirstin off by the stable building, parked the car, and walked back to the fenced-in field where Kirstin practiced. He was watching his sister mount her horse and start to canter, so he didn't notice the black car with dark windows drive into the parking lot and park behind a truck, where it would be hard to see.

Arthur stood by the fence, wondering how to get the information he had come for. Then he saw Autumn Rose's manager, a woman named Mrs. Armstrong, heading into the stables with a shovel and a pitchfork, and he knew what to do, though it wouldn't be much fun. "Hi, Mrs. Armstrong! Would you like some help with that?" He had discovered that people are much more willing to help you if you help them first.

"That's very nice of you, but I'm going to be cleaning out the stables. It's a pretty messy job and you're not really dressed for it."

Arthur winced inside, but he said, "That's OK. I'll just put fresh straw in the stalls after you clean them out. That's not too dirty."

She looked a little surprised at his eagerness to help but said, "I suppose not. Well, the help sure would be nice. Come on."

The stables were stuffy and they stank, and the dust from the hay gave Arthur sneezing fits and made his eyes itch. Other than that, though, the work wasn't too bad. After they had been at it for about ten minutes, Arthur said, "So, how did Autumn Rose get its name anyway?"

"Pretty name, isn't it?" said Mrs. Armstrong as she dumped a pitchfork-full of dirty straw into a big wheelbarrow. "I think the name came from Jean-Luc St. Vincent, the man who founded Autumn Rose." She stopped working and leaned on her pitchfork. Her tan, weathered face wore a slightly dreamy smile, and her eyes had a faraway look, as if she were remembering something pleasant from a long time ago. "I haven't seen him in a long time. A very long time. He ran this place up until about ten years ago, when he sold it to the Butlers. Nicest man you ever met, and he had this great French accent. Saddest day around here was when he sold the business and bought a place out by the Fox River."

This is great, thought Arthur, *I've already got the answer to one of the two questions, and Kirstin's lesson isn't even over yet.* "Speaking of Frenchmen," he said, "have you ever heard of Pierre LeGrand?"

Mrs. Armstrong's smile disappeared, and she looked at him with hard, suspicious eyes. "Why do you ask?"

Arthur was surprised and taken aback. "What's the matter?"

"There were some foreigners here yesterday asking that same question." She stood with her arms crossed and a stern look on her face, like a teacher who's caught a kid shooting spitballs. "I didn't like the look of them, and they wouldn't tell me their names. Are you and Kirstin doing detective work for them?"

"No."

"So why are you asking about this Mr. LeGrand?"

"I, uh, well . . ." He couldn't think of a way to hide what he was up to without lying, which he wouldn't do, so he stopped and decided whether he should tell the truth or say nothing at all. His family had known Mrs. Armstrong ever since Kirstin had started riding when she was eight. They had always trusted Mrs. Armstrong, so he decided to trust her now. "Well, this woman called Kirstin and me and asked us to find out whether anyone here knows anything about Pierre LeGrand. Officer MacGregor of the Elmhurst Police Department is good friends with someone who works for her, and from what he told us, it doesn't sound like his friend would have anything to do with the men who bothered you."

Mrs. Armstrong's face relaxed some. "So the police know what you're doing then?"

Arthur nodded. "In fact, Officer MacGregor is the one who referred the case to us."

Her face relaxed further. "Well, then I suppose it's all right." Her smile returned. "I'm sorry I snapped at you, Arthur. It's just that those men gave me a scare. They were bad characters.

You could tell just by looking at them." She frowned as she remembered.

"Well, I don't know anything about this Mr. LeGrand," she continued, "and neither does anyone else here. The day after those men showed up, I asked everyone who works here, and they all said no."

"Thanks," said Arthur, tugging on his lip as he thought. He didn't like the sound of mysterious men being mixed up in this, particularly men who could scare Mrs. Armstrong. She was a no-nonsense lady. He had heard that she used to break wild horses in Montana when she was young, and he had never seen any horse or student give her trouble after one angry word from her. Anyone who could scare her must be bad news. He looked at his watch. "Whoops!" he exclaimed. "Kirstin's lesson ended ten minutes ago. I'll bet she's waiting for me." He hurried out to find his sister.

Kirstin was standing by the car. She looked scared. "I think someone's been watching us!" she said when he got close. "I saw a dark car I didn't recognize leave just as I was finishing my lesson. And look at that!" She pointed to a spot in the shadows near their car. There were two footprints in the dirt surrounded by at least half a dozen fresh cigarette butts. One of them was still smoking. Arthur saw something on the ground and picked it up. It was a crumpled cigarette package. There was writing on it in a language he didn't understand, but near the bottom in small letters were the words "Produit du Vietnam." A chill ran through him, and the muscles in his shoulders tensed. Someone from Vietnam had been standing there long enough to smoke more than six cigarettes, and that person had just left. Kirstin was right, they *were* being watched.

CHAPTER 4

QUESTIONS

As soon as they were in the car, Arthur told Kirstin what he had seen and what Mrs. Armstrong had said. "And I'm ninety percent sure that one of the men who scared Mrs. Armstrong was the one smoking cigarettes and watching us," he concluded.

Kirstin shivered and nodded. "And *I'm* ninety-nine percent sure that at least one of them was in that car I saw pull out of the parking lot at the end of my lesson." Her eyes grew wide with fright. "Do you think they're following us?"

"Look back there and see," said Arthur, gesturing to the rear window.

Kirstin adjusted her mirror so she could look back without turning around. There was a dark car right behind them! She gasped. Then she saw another dark car three cars back, then another in the lane beside them. Which one was the car from the parking lot? Was it any of them? She looked hard and tried to remember exactly what the car in the parking lot had looked like, but she couldn't. "I'm sorry, Arthur," she said, twisting her purse strap in her hands, "I just don't know. I guess I didn't take a very good look at it."

Arthur groaned. "So they could be right behind us, and we have no way of knowing."

"I guess so," said Kirstin unhappily. "I'm sorry."

"It's OK. But the thought of those guys maybe being behind us gives me the creeps."

"Me too," said Kirstin. She sneaked another look at her mirror, trying to catch a glimpse of the drivers of the cars behind them. The afternoon sun was on their windshields, though, and the glare kept her from seeing anything. "What should we do?"

"Good question." He thought for a moment, then shrugged and said, "I'm open to suggestions."

"Let's try an experiment," said Kirstin. "Make a right turn at the next street."

"That isn't the way home."

"I know. We'll see if anyone follows us."

"Good idea! I should've thought of that!" He turned right at the next street while Kirstin carefully watched behind them in the mirror outside her door. One of the dark cars also made a right turn. It was black and had tinted windows, giving it a sinister look. She shivered.

"Make another right," she said. Arthur turned right again, and again the black car followed. "Do it again," she said in a tense voice. "He's still back there!" Arthur made a third right turn and a fourth—and so did the car behind them!

Arthur looked in the rearview mirror and took a deep breath. "Well, we just drove in a circle. He's definitely following us. We'll drive straight to the police station. There's no way he'll follow us there. Then we'll talk to Officer MacGregor and ask him if we can give Marie a collect call from his phone. I've got some questions to ask her before we do anything more on this case." He glanced in the mirror again and saw the black car still behind them. "We got more than we bargained for when we took this job."

The hair stood up on the back of Arthur's neck as he drove, and his palms were wet with nervous sweat. The mystery car followed them all the way to the police station, slowing down when they slowed down and speeding up when they sped up. When they turned into the station parking lot, the car drove slowly past, then turned a corner and disappeared. "Whew!" said Kirstin in relief. "I'm glad to see the last of him!"

"I'm pretty sure we haven't," said Arthur with a frown, "and that worries me. Also, he wasn't real subtle about following us. I'll bet he was trying to scare us off the case."

Two minutes later, they were in Officer MacGregor's office. They told him what had happened and what Mrs. Armstrong had said. His broad face became concerned as he listened to their story, and he jotted down notes as they talked. "Did you write down the license plate number of that car?" he asked when they finished. They hadn't. "Oh, well. Nothing we can do about that now. I'm going to open a police file on this," he said. "I think I'll want to be more involved in this case from now on.

"You two go ahead and call this Marie from my phone and I'll listen in." He paused and looked at them apologetically, as if he was sorry for what he was about to say. "Then I may have to ask you kids to stop investigating this. I don't want you getting hurt."

"We'll be careful," said Arthur reassuringly, but Officer MacGregor did not look reassured. That worried Arthur, and he hoped there was some way they could stay on the case. He had just gotten started and had so many unanswered questions.

What were those two men up to? Who was Pierre LeGrand? Why was everybody looking for him? And what did the Autumn Rose have to do with all this? If Marie wasn't willing to tell him today, he might never get answers if he had to drop the case.

He pushed all his questions to the back of his mind and dialed the number Marie had given them. "Allo, allo?" a woman's voice said in French.

"Um, hello. This is Arthur Davis," said Arthur uncertainly. "Is this Marie?"

"Yes, it is," she said, switching to English. "Hello, Arthur. What have you discovered?"

"Well," he said, "Autumn Rose got its name from its founder. I don't remember his name, but he was French. It wasn't Pierre LeGrand, though. Nobody there had heard of him."

"Excellent!" exclaimed Marie. "You and your sister do good work! I'll have the five hundred dollars delivered to you within a week. Now you must find that Frenchman who named the horse farm and find out why he named it that."

"Wait a minute," said Arthur. "There are some things we need to know. First—"

"I'll pay you another two hundred dollars," interrupted Marie. "That's all you need to know."

"No, wait," insisted Arthur. "For starters, we need to know why someone who smokes Vietnamese cigarettes was watching us at Autumn Rose today and why two foreign men were there yesterday asking about Pierre LeGrand."

There were a few seconds of silence. Then Marie said something in French that Arthur didn't understand, and based on her tone, he was glad he didn't. "Why didn't you tell me this first?" she demanded sharply. Arthur was about to answer when she said, "No, don't say anything more! This line must be bugged; that's the only explanation for those men! Didn't that occur to you?"

"We're not calling from our house," Arthur said defensively, thinking she meant that the mystery men had bugged his family's phone.

"Not your phone, mine!" snapped Marie. "How do you think they knew about Autumn Rose or you?"

"How can I know anything if you never tell us anything?" Arthur protested. "We can't investigate a case right unless we know what's going on!"

Marie was silent again for a moment. "What number are you at?"

"630-555-5203," said Arthur, reading from Officer MacGregor's phone.

"Stay there," said Marie. "Someone will call you." Then she hung up and the line went dead.

CHAPTER 5

ANSWERS

Fifteen minutes later, the phone rang. Arthur picked it up. "Hello?"

"Mr. Davis, what are you doing sitting in Frank MacGregor's chair?" demanded a man's voice with an Asian accent.

The hair on the back of Arthur's neck stood up. *How does he know where I'm sitting?* "I, uh, I . . ." Arthur stammered in shock.

The man laughed. "I recognized the phone number. This is Jack Nguyen. Madame Dragonfly asked me to call you."

"Madame Dragonfly?" asked Arthur, confused.

"That is what most people call her," said Mr. Nguyen, "though perhaps she has used a different name with you. That would be understandable."

"Why?" asked Arthur.

"She is a powerful woman, and she has powerful enemies who are always spying on her. She called you from a line she thought was safe, but she used a different name in case it wasn't."

At last, thought Arthur, *someone who actually answers questions and doesn't just tell us we don't need to know!* He motioned for Kirstin to come over and held the receiver so she could listen too. "OK," he said. "So why are we investigating Autumn Rose? And who is Pierre LeGrand?"

"Ah, you come to the heart of the matter," said Mr. Nguyen. "Monsieur LeGrand was—and perhaps still is—Madame Dragonfly's father. He disappeared when the Communists overran Saigon. Some say he died and some say he escaped, but no one knows. When he vanished, a very valuable treasure called the Autumn Rose vanished with him. He had promised to give it to Madame when she was ready, but he never did, and she has heard nothing from him since just before Saigon fell.

"Then one day just two weeks ago, she happened to hear of a horse farm in America called Autumn Rose. Her father had loved horses, so a horse farm with that name was certainly worth looking into. She asked me to investigate it without attracting attention, so I called my old friend Frank MacGregor, who recommended you and your sister."

"I'm here too," said Kirstin. "Well, that explains a lot, but who are these men who've been following us and snooping around Autumn Rose? And who bugged Mar—uh, Madame Dragonfly's phone?"

"I wish I knew," said Mr. Nguyen. "She says she has never told anyone about the Autumn Rose. Perhaps one of her rivals tapped her phone for some other reason, overheard her conversation with you by chance, and sent agents to America to find out what Madame Dragonfly was doing." He paused. "But I don't think so. It's not cheap or easy to get people into America from Vietnam, and no one I can think of would bother doing it without knowing more."

"So someone knows more," said Arthur.

"Yes, someone does," said Mr. Nguyen, "but I do not know who."

"What is the Autumn Rose?" asked Kirstin.

"I think it's a pearl of some sort. I don't know anything beyond that, but I believe Madame Dragonfly does," said Mr. Nguyen. "She told me that it was worth more than two million dollars in 1975, the last time anybody saw it. It's probably worth a lot more today."

"Wow!" gasped Kirstin. Even two million dollars was more money than either she or Arthur could imagine. That really was a pearl of great price!

Just then Arthur remembered something. "Jean-Luc St. Vincent!" he exclaimed.

"What?" said Mr. Nguyen.

"Have you ever heard of Jean-Luc St. Vincent?" asked Arthur. "He's the one who named the horse farm 'Autumn Rose.'"

"No," said Mr. Nguyen after a moment, "no, I don't believe I've ever heard that name. He does sound like someone you should talk to, though . . . if you're still on the case, that is."

Kirstin looked at Arthur. He bit his lip, scrunched his eyebrows together, and thought hard for a few seconds. "I think we know enough for now. We can call you back if we have more questions, right?"

"Of course, of course!" said Mr. Nguyen happily. "You can call too, Frank."

Officer MacGregor chuckled and uncovered the mouthpiece of the receiver he had been using to listen in on the conversation. "Lucky guess, Jack," he said.

"Guess?" said Mr. Nguyen with a laugh. "Two young detectives are sitting in your office and using your phone to make international calls. It didn't take much guessing to figure out that you were listening."

Officer MacGregor chuckled again. "Sharp as ever, Jack. Where can we reach you?"

"You can ring me at 33-1-42-52-63-24 for the next two weeks," Mr. Nguyen answered. "I'll give you another number after that if the case is still open."

"We'll let you know as soon as we're able to talk to Mr. St. Vincent," said Arthur, looking carefully at Officer MacGregor for any sign of protest. There was none. That meant they were still on the case!

CHAPTER 6

JEAN-LUC ST. VINCENT

The next morning, Arthur and Kirstin called Mrs. Armstrong, who gave them Mr. St. Vincent's phone number. She had already talked to him about the events of the past few days, and he had said he would be happy to talk to them. They called him and arranged a meeting for later that afternoon. After the incident the day before, their mom insisted on driving them, though she did agree to let them handle the interview themselves while she did some shopping in a nearby farm town.

Mr. St. Vincent lived about twenty miles west of Glen Ellyn, in the middle of miles and miles of corn and soybean farms. He had thirty acres of pasture on which he raised a few horses. Some of them he sold, but the best ones he gave away to people he knew would appreciate and care for them.

He was waiting for them on his porch when they came. He was a short, wiry man with silver hair and friendly blue eyes. A plate of oatmeal cookies and a pitcher of lemonade sat waiting for them on a wicker table surrounded by plastic chairs. Soon the plate and pitcher were empty and Arthur, Kirstin, and Mr. St. Vincent were talking and laughing like old friends. When the conversation turned to horses, Kirstin saw her opportunity. "Oh, wow," she gushed, "it must be so great to be able to live with all these beautiful horses and ride them whenever you want!" She had found that acting like a wide-eyed, excited little girl was an especially good technique for getting information from older people.

"Yes, it is nice," he said. "It's peaceful and exciting at the same time, if you know what I mean."

Kirstin's blond ponytail bobbed as she nodded. "That's how horses make me feel too. How did you get to do something so fun your whole life?"

"I didn't do it my *whole* life," he said with a grandfatherly smile. "I didn't start until I came to America in 1975. I didn't really know what to do with myself, but I had some money and I liked horses, so I started Autumn Rose."

"That's such a pretty name!" said Kirstin. "How did you think it up?"

"It came from a man named Pierre LeGrand," he said. "I think you asked Fran Armstrong about him." Kirstin and Arthur snuck excited glances at each other. "He and I knew each other in Vietnam before the Communist takeover. He had a great treasure named the Autumn Rose. I liked the name so much, I gave it to my horse farm." He looked at them carefully, studying their faces. "By the way, why are you two so interested in it and Pierre?"

"A client has asked us to look into it," answered Arthur.

"If you don't mind my asking, who is your client?" Mr. St. Vincent asked.

"I don't mind your asking," said Arthur, "but I can't tell you without our client's permission. I hope you understand."

"Certainly, certainly," Mr. St. Vincent said, stroking his chin thoughtfully.

"Where's Mr. LeGrand now?" asked Arthur, leaning forward in his seat.

"Gone," answered Mr. St. Vincent with a sigh. "The Communists were closing in on Saigon, and he and I were supposed to escape together on a Thai cargo ship at night. I made it safely, but he didn't. He was in a motorboat coming out to the ship. The night was very dark, so he must not have seen the South Vietnamese patrol boat near him. Suddenly, the patrol boat turned on its spotlight and ordered him to stop. He knew they would throw him in jail or worse, so he opened the throttle on his motor and tried to escape. He would have made it, but there were mines in the harbor, and he hit one."

"And that killed him?" asked Arthur.

Mr. St. Vincent looked at him. "Those mines were intended to sink ships. Imagine what they would do to a motorboat."

"Oh," said Arthur, feeling a little foolish. "I'm sorry."

"What happened to the Autumn Rose?" asked Kirstin.

Mr. St. Vincent shrugged. "I assume it was in the boat with him. He never told me what it was, but I think it was small enough to carry. I never heard anything more about it after that—until now, that is."

"So why would the men in the patrol boat have arrested him?" asked Kirstin.

"Oh, because he was a thief," said Mr. St. Vincent, arching his eyebrows slightly in surprise. "I thought you knew that. He was a very successful cat burglar, the best in Saigon. The police overlooked his crimes for years because he also worked as a government agent, breaking into the homes of suspected communists in Saigon to look for incriminating evidence. He retired from his life of crime quite suddenly, though, and went to work for a missionary. Then the government stopped protecting him, and his enemies—he had quite a few—came looking for him."

Just then, a horse walked into view in the pasture just beyond the porch. He was a dappled gray Arabian with a long silky mane that shone in the afternoon sun. Kirstin's eyes grew round when she saw him. "Oh, he's beautiful!" she exclaimed. "Do you think I could ride him?"

Mr. St. Vincent smiled at her excitement, but shook his head. "I'm taking him and his mother to a show in about an hour, and I'll need to brush them down and get them ready." He paused for a moment in thought, then snapped his fingers. "I do take them all for a morning ride each day, and you're welcome to ride him tomorrow morning."

"Great!" said Kirstin. "When should I be here?"

"Well, I start taking them out at seven," said Mr. St. Vincent. "I hope that's not too early for you."

"It's not," said Kirstin cheerfully, but Arthur winced. There was a good chance he would have to drive her, and he *hated* getting up early.

"Good," he said. "I'll see you then." This, of course, was a signal for them to leave so he could get his horses ready for the show. They said good-bye and called their mom on her cell phone to come pick them up. All of them were in good moods as they drove along the gravel road heading away from Mr. St. Vincent's house. Mrs. Davis had found some beautiful antique earrings in a little shop and had bought some delicious looking fresh corn for dinner that night. Arthur and Kirstin were happy to have solved the mystery and earned two hundred dollars for a pleasant afternoon's work, and Kirstin was excited about going riding the next morning. None of them noticed the red car parked on the side of the road about fifty yards from the end of Mr. St. Vincent's driveway, or the two Asian men sitting in it.

By the time they reached the highway, Kirstin noticed that her brother wasn't saying much. She looked over and saw that he was lost in thought. "What is it?" she asked.

"I was thinking about those guys who were following us."

Kirstin quickly looked in her mirror, but didn't see any dark cars, only a bright red one. She didn't pay any attention to it, though, because it looked nothing like the car that had followed them before. "Well, they're not back there," she said with relief. "What about them?"

"That's what I'm wondering," said Arthur. "Are they just going to disappear now?"

"Why not? Sooner or later, they'll figure out that Pierre LeGrand is dead and that the Autumn Rose was either blasted to bits or is at the bottom of some harbor in Vietnam. Then they'll leave."

Arthur stared out the window, absently watching the road and the rows of ripening corn as he chewed over his sister's logic. He couldn't find any holes in it. "I suppose you're right," he said at last. Still, he couldn't shake the feeling that they had not seen the last of the mystery men.

Kirstin woke her brother at six the next morning. He groaned and looked at her with bleary, unhappy eyes. She was already showered and dressed. "Come on!" she said. "I don't want to be late!"

"Yeah? Well, *I* don't want to be awake," he retorted. "Why can't Mom drive you?"

"She says she thinks it's safe for us to go alone now. Also, I don't think she wants to be awake either."

Arthur groaned again, sat up, and stretched his long arms. His thick, unruly brown hair stuck out from the side of his head like a horn.

"You won't have time to shower," said Kirstin, noticing his hair. "You should wear a hat, though." Arthur looked like he was about to get mad, so she quickly added, "I'll run down and fix you some breakfast."

"Thanks," he mumbled as she ducked out of his room.

Twenty-five minutes later, they were driving west. They made good time and reached Mr. St. Vincent's house at 6:55. As she got out of the car, Kirstin shivered. It wasn't cold, but it was still nearly dark and a thick fog from the Fox River made the old wooden house look haunted and menacing. "It wouldn't look nearly so spooky if he just turned on some lights," she said to herself as she walked up the path to the door. Then she stopped. Why weren't there any lights on? Mr. St. Vincent must be up, and it was still too dark to be doing things around the house with the lights off.

She cautiously walked up to the door and pressed the doorbell. No sound came. *The power must be out,* she thought with relief. That would explain why the house was dark. She knocked on the door, and it swung open at her touch. She reached for the knob, but stopped. The bolt had been sawed through! That was why the door had opened when she knocked. She stepped back, eyes wide with fright, then turned and ran back to the car.

CHAPTER 7

OFF THE CASE

"What is it?" Arthur asked when Kirstin came sprinting back.

"Someone broke into the house!" she gasped. "And no one answered when I knocked!"

"Get in the car!" said Arthur tensely. "We're getting out of here!" He turned on the engine as she got in, turned the car around, and sped down the driveway. Loose gravel sprayed away from the wheels as the car accelerated. "Call 911," he said as they turned onto the street.

Kirstin took out her phone and dialed with trembling hands. It seemed to take forever to explain who they were, where they were, and why the police needed to come, but the dispatcher finally said the police would be there in five minutes. Kirstin turned off the phone and asked, "Do you think we should go back?"

Arthur took a deep breath and blew it out. "Yeah, we probably should. It should be safe now that the police are coming." He turned the car around and headed back the way they had come. The sun had fully risen by now, and there were other cars on the road as people drove to work, making the drive back to the house seem eerily normal, but still breathlessly frightening. Who knew what they would find at the house? That question hung heavy over them as they drove.

Kirstin finally broke the silence. "Do you think Mr. St. Vincent is OK?"

Arthur shrugged. "I don't know. I hope so. Let's pray for him." And they did.

Two police cars were already at Mr. St. Vincent's house when Arthur and Kirstin turned into his driveway. Two policemen were walking toward the house with their pistols drawn while two more crouched behind the cars holding shotguns. One of the officers motioned for Arthur and Kirstin to stop and ran over, holding his shotgun at the ready the whole time. "Who are you and what are you doing here?" he demanded.

"We're Arthur and Kirstin Davis," answered Arthur nervously. "We're the ones who called 911. We came back to see if we could help."

"This is a police situation now, and it's very dangerous," said the officer as he watched the house intently. "You'll have to leave." The policeman turned and ran back behind his squad car in a crouch, as if he expected to be shot at any second.

"Is Mr. St. Vincent all right?" Kirstin called after him.

"Move!" the policeman shouted back, pointing back down the driveway. They moved. Arthur put the car in reverse and pulled back onto the street. They realized there was really nothing more for them to do there, so they headed home. They had lots of questions as they drove, but no sure answers, just worrying possibilities. Had Mr. St. Vincent been killed by those men? Were they next? What had they gotten themselves into?

When they reached home, Arthur nearly crashed into Officer MacGregor's car. The Davises had a long, winding driveway with bushes and small trees growing along it, which could make it hard to see parked cars if one wasn't careful. Arthur usually was careful, but he had a lot on his mind that morning, and he wasn't really watching where he was going. He turned the last curve going a little too fast and boom! there was the police car just a few feet in front of him. "Look out!" screamed Kirstin. Arthur slammed on the brakes and screeched to a halt with his front bumper just inches from Officer MacGregor's!

Once the car stopped, Arthur and Kirstin caught their breath before getting out. That had been a close call! Officer MacGregor got out of his car first and stood waiting for them with an amused smile. "Whew!" said Arthur. "At least he doesn't look mad at us!"

Kirstin arched her eyebrows at the word "us," but only said, "Yeah, and he wouldn't be smiling if he had bad news about Mr. St. Vincent."

"We'll see," said Arthur as they got out of the car.

"Does your detective agency make enough money to buy me a new squad car?" Officer MacGregor asked with a laugh.

"Uh, not really," answered Arthur, who was too tense to think of anything clever to say. He ran his fingers through his hair, revealing armpits wet with nervous sweat.

"I didn't think so," said Officer MacGregor, who now looked a little sorry for Arthur. "Well, don't worry about it. I hear you've had a pretty exciting morning, so I can see why you might be a little distracted. Why don't you park your car and get into mine. I'll need to take you two down to the station to ask you some questions about Mr. St. Vincent."

Arthur let Kirstin ride in the passenger seat of the police car and got in the backseat. When he went to close the door, though, he discovered that there was no handle on the inside. Officer MacGregor shut the door for him. "How am I supposed to get out when we get to the station?" Arthur asked.

"You're not," said Officer MacGregor with a grin. "We keep suspects back there. Do you think we want them to be able to open the door and get out whenever we pull up to a stop sign?"

As soon as Officer MacGregor got in the car, Kirstin asked the question that had been on her and Arthur's minds for the past hour, "Is Mr. St. Vincent all right?" Arthur leaned forward to the wire mesh that separated the backseat from the front, eager to hear the policeman's response.

Officer MacGregor frowned and shrugged his thick shoulders. "We don't know for sure. The house was empty when the Saint Charles police got there. No burglars, and no Mr. St. Vincent. He seems to have disappeared. No blood, no footprints or drag marks; he's just gone. Maybe they kidnapped him."

"Why would they do that?" asked Arthur.

The big policeman shrugged again. "No idea yet. Regular robbery doesn't seem to be the motive, though. His place was torn apart pretty good, but nothing seems to have been stolen. The TV is still there. So are a lot of silver, an expensive looking computer, and a new car. Whoever did this was looking for something specific. Maybe they couldn't find it and took Mr. St. Vincent so they could force him to show them where it is."

"Who do you think did this?" asked Kirstin as innocently as she could.

"I've got a pretty good idea, and I think you do too," he answered. "I think your friends from the horse farm are playing a little out of your league now."

Arthur's heart dropped. "What do you mean?" he asked.

"I mean that this really isn't something for youngsters like you two to be mixed up in." Officer MacGregor glanced at them apologetically. "I'll keep you in the loop about what's going on in the case, but this is a police matter now, and I can't have you in the middle of it."

Arthur slumped back against the vinyl of his seat and Kirstin winced. "So you're telling us we're off the case," Arthur said in a monotone.

Officer MacGregor nodded sadly. "I'm afraid so."

CHAPTER 8

FINGERPRINTS

O nce they reached the police station, there was a lot to do. After they called to touch base with their parents, they answered numerous questions from Officer MacGregor and a policeman from the Saint Charles Police Department, which was mostly handling the investigation. After that, all four of them called Mr. Nguyen to tell him what had happened and see if he knew anything useful, which unfortunately he didn't. Then Arthur and Kirstin had their fingerprints taken so that they could be compared to any prints found at Mr. St. Vincent's house. If the police found fingerprints that did not belong to Mr. St. Vincent, Arthur, or Kirstin, then they probably belonged to whoever broke into the house.

They didn't finish at the police station until nearly 1:30, by which time Arthur and Kirstin were positively starving. Officer MacGregor guessed as much and offered to take them out for burgers and shakes, an offer they eagerly accepted. He insisted on paying for their food, and they could tell he really felt bad about taking them off the case. He wasn't willing to budge on his decision, though, and neither Arthur's polite arguments nor Kirstin's big, sad blue eyes had any effect.

After Officer MacGregor dropped them off at home, they

spent the rest of the day trying not to think about the case. Arthur went to soccer practice and stayed late to work on his corner kicks. Kirstin went to the pool with her friends and then spent the evening fiddling with some new e-mail software she had found on the Internet. They were tired when they went to bed, but neither of them was able to go to sleep for a long time.

At ten the next morning, the phone rang. Arthur yelled "I've got it!" from the kitchen, and Kirstin yelled the same thing from the family room. They each grabbed a receiver and said "Hello?" simultaneously.

"Uh, Arthur? Kirstin?" said a confused man's voice, a voice that they both recognized.

"We're both here, Officer MacGregor," said Arthur. "Do you want us to come to your office, or is it safe to talk on the phone?"

"The phone is fine," said the policeman. "I've got an anti-bugging gadget on my phone now that would tell me if anyone else was listening in. Actually, it might not matter if they did. There's not much to report, but I figured I'd give you a call anyway to let you know what's going on."

"And?" asked Kirstin eagerly.

"Well, like I said, we haven't found much. The only fingerprints that we found came from the two of you and from what must be Mr. St. Vincent, though we can't find his prints in the FBI database. The only interesting news is that we weren't the only ones taking prints in his house. We found sprinklings of talcum powder and traces of adhesive from cellophane tape."

"Meaning whoever broke into that house was using the powder to find prints and the tape to pick them up," said Arthur.

"Right," said the policeman.

"Hmmm," said Arthur. "I wonder what they were up to. Did they take prints from a lot of places in the house?"

"Just two," said Officer MacGregor. "And as far as we can tell, the only prints they were interested in were Mr. St. Vincent's."

"That's weird," said Arthur. "Why would they care about his fingerprints?"

"Should his prints have been in the FBI database?" Kirstin asked suddenly.

"I suppose so," said Officer MacGregor. "When he moved to the U.S., he must have either become a citizen or gotten a green card, which would let him stay here and work even though he was a citizen of another country. Either way, he would have been fingerprinted, and those prints should have gone into the FBI's database. This is the federal government we're talking about, though, so just because something should have happened doesn't mean it did. Also, it's possible your friend was an illegal alien, in which case his prints wouldn't be in the system unless he was arrested and fingerprinted by the police."

"Would you find his prints if they were in the database under a different name?" she asked.

"Yes," said the officer. "Why?"

"I've got an idea," answered Kirstin. "Are there any other databases you could search that would include France or Vietnam?"

"I suppose I could check the Interpol database," he answered.

"Could you do that, please?" she asked urgently.

"Well, it'll cost something," Officer MacGregor said hesitantly, "but you've usually got pretty good hunches. Hold on a minute." Arthur and Kirstin could hear him typing in the background. "There," he said, "this should be pretty quick. Now, Kirstin, who exactly are you expecting to be the owner of those prints?"

"I was wondering the same thing," chimed in Arthur, "though I've got an idea of what you're thinking."

"Well—" said Kirstin, but before she could answer, Officer MacGregor interrupted her with a low whistle. "Who is it?" she asked, guessing that the computer had finished its search.

"Nice work, Kirstin!" he said. "Those fingerprints belong to a Mr. Pierre LeGrand. There's a picture of him here. Let me e-mail it to you."

Two minutes later, Arthur and Kirstin were huddled together in front of the computer, waiting breathlessly for the picture to come. It came! Then they had to wait for seconds that seemed to take forever as the computer opened the picture. Slowly a grainy black-and-white image took shape on the screen. It showed a young, handsome man with dark hair and shrewd, hard eyes, but it was unmistakably an old picture of the man they knew as Jean-Luc St. Vincent!

Five minutes later, they were on a three-way conference call with Officer MacGregor and Mr. Nguyen. "Such a nice surprise to hear from you again so soon," Mr. Nguyen said politely. "Is there more news?"

"Go ahead, Kirstin," said Officer MacGregor. "You figured it out."

Kirstin was caught by surprise. She had thought Officer MacGregor would take the lead because he was an adult and because she and Arthur were officially off the case. "We, uh, like we . . . ," she fumbled, trying to think of how to best lead up to what happened. Then she gave up and blurted out, "Mr. St. Vincent is really Pierre LeGrand. He's still alive!"

"*Zut alors!*" Mr. Nguyen exclaimed in shock. Then there was silence on the phone for several seconds as he absorbed the magnitude of the news. "Have you received any ransom demands?" he asked.

"We haven't heard anything," said Officer MacGregor.

"I wonder who they would call to make ransom demands," said Arthur. "I suppose it would depend on whether they know who he really is."

"I must tell Madame immediately," said Mr. Nguyen. "I will call you back shortly. Are you all in Frank's office?"

"Just call me here and I'll hook everybody in," said Officer MacGregor, and they all hung up.

Arthur and Kirstin waited for the phone to ring again. And waited. After about fifteen minutes, Arthur decided to go to the bathroom, which is one of the best ways to make the phone ring. Sure enough, as soon as he shut the door, it rang. "I'll get it!" called Kirstin as Arthur hurried back out. A few seconds later, she called, "It's Officer MacGregor!"

Arthur picked up the phone and said, "Hi, Officer."

"Hi, Arthur," said Officer MacGregor. "Hold on a sec." There was a clicking noise, then he said, "Jack, you there?"

"I'm here," confirmed Mr. Nguyen.

"Good," said Officer MacGregor, "then we should have everyone. Go ahead, Jack."

"Madame Dragonfly is coming to America," he said. "She asks that you meet her for breakfast tomorrow morning at seven at the Oak Brook Hilton."

"Um, I'm not sure it will be necessary for Arthur and Kirstin to come," said Officer MacGregor. "This is an active police matter now, so they're not on the case anymore."

"Ah," said Mr. Nguyen. "I see. Well, Madame has specifically invited them, so I believe it *is* necessary for them to come. Even if they are no longer on the case, I am sure she would like to meet them and treat them to breakfast."

"We'd like to meet her too," added Kirstin, who was intensely curious to see what this mysterious woman looked like.

Officer MacGregor chuckled good-naturedly, but he did not entirely like the sound of Mr. Nguyen's comments. It sounded like this woman might be a headache to deal with. "I suppose there's no harm in a little breakfast," he said. "By the way, why does the fact that this 'Madame Dragonfly' invited them make it 'necessary' for them to come?" he added in a carefully casual voice.

Mr. Nguyen laughed. "You will be able to answer that question for yourself once you meet her."

CHAPTER 9

ENTER THE DRAGONFLY

Arthur and Kirstin felt a little intimidated as they walked into the Oak Brook Hilton. The parking lot held limousines, luxury cars like Lexuses and BMWs, and the Davises' slightly rusty five-year-old Honda. "At least I don't have to worry about anybody stealing Mom's car," Arthur had remarked as he parked it next to a beautiful new Cadillac that was worth at least eight times as much as their Honda.

The white and red marble floor of the hotel lobby was scattered with elegant Persian rugs. The lobby furniture all seemed to be made out of mahogany wood, leather, and brass. Officer MacGregor sat waiting for them in a big leather armchair that creaked whenever he moved. The chair was well padded, but he looked as uncomfortable as Arthur and Kirstin felt. His off-the-rack jacket and slightly loud tie were plainly out of place in a room of elegant people in well-tailored suits and business dresses.

We stick out like sore thumbs, thought Kirstin as they walked over to meet Officer MacGregor. *Maybe we're supposed to,* she realized. *Maybe Madame Dragonfly is meeting us here because we'll be in her world, not ours.*

Officer MacGregor got up (accompanied by a loud creak

from the chair) as Arthur and Kirstin approached. "Morning," he greeted them as he adjusted his tie and jacket. "She left a message at the front desk that we're supposed to meet her in a private dining room on the third floor, so let's head up."

As they rode up in the elevator, Officer MacGregor said, "By the way, since we're talking about a police investigation, why don't you two let me take the lead." The elevator doors opened, and they walked down the hall to conference room 3. A very large Asian man with red eyes who needed a shave was standing outside the door and trying, unsuccessfully, to keep from yawning. "Rough flight?" asked Officer MacGregor with a friendly smile.

The man nodded and groaned. "We left sixteen hours ago and just get into hotel at six."

Officer MacGregor shook his head in sympathy. "Sounds pretty bad. I'm Lieutenant Frank MacGregor, and these are Arthur and Kirstin Davis. I believe we are expected."

"Yes, you are," said the man. "Please go in." He politely opened the door for them.

They entered a small, square conference room with a large round table in the middle of the floor. Four places were set for breakfast, and a waitress stood to one side, ready to take their orders. A muscular European looking man with a wrinkled shirt sat in a chair in one of the back corners of the room. Like the Asian man outside, he looked like he badly needed a long nap. Sitting behind the table was a small woman who appeared to be in her early forties. She had elegant Asian features and striking blue eyes. She wore a stylish black suit with a green scarf and a matching jade broach shaped like a dragonfly. Unlike her travel companions, she gave no hint of being tired from her long trip. Her eyes were clear and alert, and Kirstin noticed that they had the same hard shrewdness that she had seen in the eyes of Pierre LeGrand in the old picture that Officer MacGregor had e-mailed. "Thank you for coming on such short notice," she said with a smile. "Please, sit down."

Once they were seated, the waitress took their orders and left. Arthur, Kirstin, and Officer MacGregor had been expecting introductions and some small-talk to begin their meeting, but Madame Dragonfly got straight to business. She opened a leather notebook, took out a pen, and said, "Please give me a full report on where the investigation stands."

She had spoken to Arthur, but Officer MacGregor answered. "I'm sorry, ma'am, but there's not a lot to report." Madame Dragonfly watched him closely and took notes as he talked. "Whoever broke into your father's home was very careful not to leave evidence. There were no fingerprints, shoe prints, hair, or other potential identifiers at the crime scene. In fact, it looks like they were actually *looking for* fingerprints, but we haven't yet figured out why. Maybe they weren't sure who he was and needed to confirm his identity.

"We also haven't found any witnesses, and I doubt we will. Mr. LeGrand lived in a pretty secluded area. His closest neighbor is almost half a mile away—that's, uh, a little less than a kilometer."

"I know," she said crisply. "Go on."

"Well," continued Officer MacGregor, "we haven't found your father, and we haven't heard from his kidnappers—"

"You're quite sure he was kidnapped, then?" She had interrupted him, but seemed not to notice.

"Well, that's our, uh, theory right now," said Officer

MacGregor uncertainly. "That's where all the evidence seems to be pointing."

"Were there any signs of a struggle?"

"It's hard to say. The house was a mess. Papers were all over the floor. Furniture had been torn apart. Holes had been knocked in the walls. That didn't all come from a struggle, but some of it might have."

"I see," Madame Dragonfly said. "And there was no ransom note, correct?"

"Correct."

"And you have received no phone calls requesting a ransom, correct?"

"Also correct," said Officer MacGregor, who felt uncomfortably like she was giving him a test and he wasn't doing very well.

"Then why do you say all the facts indicate that he was kidnapped?"

"Well, no one has seen him since the time of the break-in," said Officer MacGregor, looking at the table. He looked up at her, but dropped his eyes again to avoid her intent gaze. "Also, I understand that he may have been in possession of a very valuable pearl called the Autumn Rose. It looks like someone broke into his house looking for it. My guess is that they couldn't find it, so they tried to make your father tell them where it was. Maybe it wasn't there, so they took him with them to go get it. Maybe they took him with them so that they would have more time to get the information out of him."

At that moment, the waitress returned with their food. She spent several minutes delivering plates, filling coffee cups, and asking if everything was all right. As soon as she was gone,

Madame Dragonfly said, "I tend to agree with you, at least for the present." Officer MacGregor nodded as he consumed a large Denver omelet as fast as good manners would allow, fearing that she would start interrogating him again and that he would not have a chance to eat. That would have been a pity, because the omelet was very good. Kirstin, meanwhile, was enjoying her Belgian waffle with whipped cream and strawberries and Arthur was relishing his delicious blueberry pancakes as they listened, thankful that they weren't being grilled by this formidable woman.

"Your theory leaves one significant unanswered question," Madame Dragonfly continued after a moment. Officer MacGregor looked up nervously. "What happens to my father after the kidnappers find the Autumn Rose?"

Officer MacGregor put down his fork and took a deep breath. "Well, maybe they'll ask for a ransom."

"But maybe not," she said.

"But maybe not," repeated Officer MacGregor sadly.

She nodded gravely, but showed no emotion. "Then we'll have to find them before they find the Autumn Rose."

CHAPTER 10

BACK ON THE CASE

Madame Dragonfly finished her breakfast of melon and yogurt, pushed her plate to one side, and picked up her pen and notebook again. "Now, what are your plans for finding my father?" she asked Officer MacGregor.

The policeman swallowed the last bite of his omelet and took a sip of his coffee, which gave him a few seconds to collect his thoughts. "We've got some witnesses still to interview and we'll finish searching your father's house and property for clues. Other than that, though, there really isn't much for us to do. I'll be honest; we don't have any leads, and we aren't likely to get any. Whoever did this was very careful."

"And how about you?" she asked, turning suddenly toward Arthur and Kirstin. "What do you think we should do?"

These were the first words she had spoken to them since the beginning of the meeting, so they were a little surprised. Kirstin looked at Arthur with a gleam in her eye and the trace of a mischievous smile. Arthur had a pretty good idea of what she was thinking, and he agreed. If they played their cards right, maybe they could get back on the case. He suspected that Madame Dragonfly would be willing to help. "If they're looking for the Autumn Rose," he said, "I think our plan should be to find it first. Then they'll come to us."

Officer MacGregor frowned and opened his mouth to say something, but before he could get it out, Madame Dragonfly said, "Excellent idea! And how do you think we should do that?"

Officer MacGregor shook his head. "I'm afraid that isn't something we can put police resources into," he said. "I think it's a good idea too, but I just don't think I can sell our police department or Saint Charles on it. I can just hear the Chief now. He'll say, 'We're policemen, MacGregor, not treasure hunters!'"

Madame Dragonfly smiled like a chess player whose opponent has just made a mistake. "That's all right. My detectives" (here she gestured to Arthur and Kirstin) "and I will do the treasure hunting."

"I'm sorry, ma'am," said Officer MacGregor, "but they're no longer on the case. This is a police matter."

"I thought you just said that the police wouldn't look for the Autumn Rose," she replied.

"That's true, but, uh, . . . well," he said, but had no idea how to finish his sentence. For once, he wished she would interrupt him.

"Then the search for the Autumn Rose is not a police matter, and you have no objection to them being on the case, correct?" she asked.

"It's just that, uh, I'd be concerned for their safety."

"Don't be," said Madame Dragonfly. She gestured to the big man sitting in the corner. "Vladimir is a licensed bodyguard, and a very good one. So is Dat, who is standing outside the door."

Officer MacGregor wasn't convinced. "I'm sure these gentlemen are good at what they do, but the answer is still no. Arthur and Kirstin would be much safer at home having nothing to do with this case."

"Would they?" asked Madame Dragonfly sharply, leaning forward in her chair. "If my father can't or won't tell those men where the Autumn Rose is, they'll try these two young detectives. If that happens, their home won't be very safe, will it?" Arthur gulped and Kirstin suddenly felt a cold knot of fear in her stomach. They hadn't thought of that!

Officer MacGregor was caught, and he knew it. He smiled ruefully and said, "Maybe not. All right, they can go back on the case." He turned to Arthur and Kirstin. "But you two be careful, and you'd better not get in the way of the police investigation!"

"We won't, sir!" said Kirstin respectfully. "And don't worry. After all that's happened, we'll be super careful!" Arthur nodded in agreement.

CHAPTER 11

A DEAD END

Three days later, Arthur and Kirstin were not nearly so excited to be back on the case, even though Madame Dragonfly had agreed to pay them twenty dollars an hour, plus expenses. For one thing, they were beginning to get tired of Dat, who had been assigned to guard them. After a long talk with Madame Dragonfly and Officer MacGregor, Mr. and Mrs. Davis had agreed to let Arthur and Kirstin back on the case and had housed Dat in the spare bedroom, though they weren't happy about how things had turned out. "When we said you two could take this case, we had no idea that a week later you would need a bodyguard to protect you," Mr. Davis had commented sternly. "But then neither did you, I suppose. Well, there's not much we can do about it now, is there?" There wasn't, Arthur and Kirstin both eagerly agreed.

Dat was very polite and seemed nice, but he followed them *everywhere* and insisted that they always be together so that he could watch them both. Also, Dat smoked. He never did it in the house, but he always smelled like stale cigarettes.

This situation was particularly hard on Kirstin. She had planned to go to the pool with her friends, but had to cancel because Dat and Arthur would have had to come along. Having

Arthur there would have been bad enough (especially since two of her friends had crushes on him), but having Dat following her around like a puppy (and watching her sunbathe!) was too horrible to even think about. So instead she wound up going to Arthur's soccer practice. Half the team was playing the other half in a scrimmage. Kirstin wasn't very interested, but Dat, who turned out to be a huge soccer fan, couldn't take his eyes off the game. Kirstin tried to strike up a conversation with him, but Dat's English somehow wasn't very good if she tried to talk about anything except soccer. She was afraid that this could be a very long summer unless they solved the case soon!

Having Dat around all the time wouldn't have been so bad if they were doing something exciting, but they weren't. They had agreed that the first thing they should do was to go through the records of Autumn Rose from the years Mr. LeGrand owned it and look for clues. Mrs. Armstrong agreed to let them go through the old files. Once they got there, though, they were unpleasantly surprised to find a room full of musty, dusty old boxes stuffed with paper. There were receipts, bills, horse breeding forms, lesson plans for students, and other papers, but nothing that cracked the case open. There were no secret diaries, no keys to safe deposit boxes, and no treasure maps. There were just thousands and thousands of pieces of paper, any one of which might hold some clue, so they all had to be looked at by Arthur or Kirstin. (Dat and Vladimir were outside keeping guard and Madame Dragonfly spent much of her time in a spare office at Autumn Rose attending to other business.) And that was a very long and very boring job.

It took them six full days to go through everything, and it

would have taken a lot longer if Madame Dragonfly hadn't been there. A long, boring job can encourage those who are doing it to take lots of breaks, particularly on sunny summer days. If Arthur and Kirstin had been there by themselves, that's probably exactly what they would have done, and the job would have taken at least another three or four days.

But Arthur and Kirstin were not alone. Madame Dragonfly was there, and she certainly lived up to her name. She was always flitting from place to place keeping an eye on their work. Sometimes she would disappear for hours, talking on her digital cell phone or speaking to Mrs. Armstrong about the man she had known as Jean-Luc St. Vincent.

Just because Madame wasn't in the room with them didn't mean that they could goof off, though, as Arthur discovered on the second day of going through boxes. It was two in the afternoon, and Arthur was having trouble staying awake. Madame Dragonfly was nowhere to be seen, so he decided to take a little break to refresh himself. He had the most recent issue of *Sports Illustrated* with him, and it had an article about the new goalkeeper for the U.S. World Cup team that looked really interesting. Arthur took out the magazine and started to read. He was about halfway through the article when a voice right behind his left shoulder said, "Does it say anything about the Autumn Rose?"

Arthur nearly fell out of his chair in surprise. He turned around, and there was Madame Dragonfly standing over him with a disgusted look on her face. She sure could walk quietly when she wanted to! "I was just, uh, just—" said Arthur lamely, trying to think of an explanation.

Madame Dragonfly finished his sentence for him. "Just not

working," she said sharply, then turned on her heel and stalked off.

"Dragonflies can sure bite," said Kirstin with a grin when Madame Dragonfly was safely gone.

"They sure can," said Arthur with a grimace as he angrily threw his magazine into his backpack. They didn't take any more breaks after that.

At the end of the sixth day, they had gone through all the boxes and discovered . . . absolutely nothing! They had learned to read Mr. LeGrand's messy handwriting, and they had discovered that, based on some old pictures they found, people in the 1970s wore some very funny clothes and hairstyles. Other than that, they knew nothing more than they had when they began.

Autumn Rose had been a dead end. They had wasted six precious days there, and it seemed to Kirstin that they were now hopelessly behind in the race to find the pearl—and save Mr. LeGrand's life!

CHAPTER 12

"U MARKS THE SPOT!"

The next place to look for clues was Mr. LeGrand's house. Both the mystery men and the police had already searched it, but there was really no better place to look. Besides, Madame Dragonfly had never seen her father's home, giving them another reason to spend time there.

To Arthur's and Kirstin's surprise, Officer MacGregor did not object, even though the house was a crime scene and was still considered a potential source of evidence by the police. He would have to go with them, of course, but that was the only condition he set. He didn't even try to say "no," maybe because he had discovered that "no" was not a very effective word when dealing with Madame Dragonfly.

Mr. LeGrand's little old wooden house looked less foreboding than the last time they had seen it. Its white paint and green shutters looked warm and homey, and beds of yellow and orange daylilies were blooming under the windows. The windows were dark, though, and yellow and black police tape surrounded the house.

Once they got inside, the contrast between the cozy country home and the crime scene grew more jarring. A peaceful painting of the French countryside hung on the wall next to a gaping hole. All the kitchen drawers had been dumped on the kitchen floor, but the table was still neatly set for breakfast, and a vase held wilted lilies that had been cut from the garden. Kirstin noticed that there were three place settings on the table and carefully walked across the cluttered floor to take a closer look. "That's strange," she said to herself in a low voice. "I thought he lived by himself. Why are there three places set?" Then she realized why. Her breath caught in her throat and she started to cry.

Madame Dragonfly heard Kirstin crying and walked over. She gently put her hand on Kirstin's shoulder and said, "What's wrong?"

Kirstin took a Kleenex from her purse and wiped her eyes and nose. "I had said I would help exercise the horses first thing in the morning," Kirstin explained, "but when Arthur and I got here, we found the house broken into and him gone." She gestured at the table and started to cry again. "He was going to fix us breakfast after we were done with the horses."

Madame Dragonfly gave Kirstin's shoulder a squeeze and said, "Let's go for a walk. I think Officer MacGregor might be relieved if he had only your brother to watch." They walked out behind the house to where the horses grazed and played during the day. Mrs. Armstrong had been taking care of them since Mr. LeGrand disappeared, and she had already fed them their morning meal and let them out of their stables. Kirstin and Madame Dragonfly watched in silence for several minutes as the horses played and grazed. "Was my father a nice man?" asked Madame Dragonfly suddenly.

"What?" asked Kirstin, caught off guard.

"Did you like him?" asked Madame Dragonfly. "I know you only met him once, but what did you think of him?"

"I liked him," said Kirstin. "He seemed really nice." She thought for a moment. "He lied to us about who he was, but I guess he had a good reason for that. Look what happened as soon as someone learned his true identity. Besides, he's got great horses."

Madame Dragonfly smiled and said, "Yes, he does."

"Why are you asking me what he was like?" Kirstin asked cautiously. "Didn't you know him?"

Madame Dragonfly sighed and looked out at the horses. "I haven't seen him since I was about your age. He disappeared suddenly one night, and I never heard from him again. He said goodnight like he always did, and then he was gone the next morning. I thought he was dead until a week ago."

Kirstin tried to imagine how she would feel if her father suddenly disappeared. "That must have been so tough," she said. "Do you know why he never called or anything?"

"That's one of the things I'd like to ask him," said Madame Dragonfly with a trace of bitterness in her voice. She watched a brown yearling gallop across the field, and her eyes lost some of their hardness. "When I was a girl, I loved to ride. I could go to the stables and gallop and jump and forget about the war and . . ." she paused for a moment, as if she was about to say something and changed her mind ". . . and everything else that made me sad."

Kirstin was wondering what to say next when she saw the look on Madame Dragonfly's face change subtly, as if she were shutting a door in her heart. She glanced at her watch and was suddenly all business again. "Let's get back to work," she said. "We don't have all day." Madame Dragonfly walked back to the house at a quick pace. Kirstin followed, thinking about what she had just heard. There was a lot more to Madame Dragonfly than met the eye.

Kirstin was so lost in thought when she walked in that she almost bumped into Arthur. "Whoops!" she said. "Sorry, I didn't see you."

"That's OK," said Arthur, glancing at her distractedly. "What do you think of that?" he asked. He pointed to a large framed photograph hanging on the wall. It showed a small, forested island surrounded by bright blue water. A picturesque log cabin with a stone chimney sat in a small clearing by the water, and a path led from the cabin to a pier. A big sailboat was tied to the pier.

"It's a nice picture," said Kirstin. "I'd like to sail on that sailboat."

"Me too," said Arthur. "Or at least I'd like to take a good look at it. Look at the name on the stern."

Kirstin squinted at the picture. The sailboat was turned sideways to the camera, so she could only make out a little of the stern, and what she could see was in the shadow. "It starts with an A," she said, "then there's two I's . . . no wait, it's a U, and then there's a T. That's all I can see." She thought for a moment as Arthur watched. Then her eyes bugged out and her mouth flew open. "Autumn Rose!" she exclaimed.

Arthur smiled and nodded. "That's what I thought too. Let's tell them."

They called in Officer MacGregor and Madame Dragonfly and showed them the picture. "Good job!" said Officer MacGregor, giving Arthur a pat on the back. "I'll call the Saint Charles boys, and we'll see if we can't find the registry for that boat."

"Yes, well done," said Madame Dragonfly. "The horse farm and this house don't seem to hold any clues, but perhaps that boat does."

Officer MacGregor stroked his chin and observed, "This guy sure likes that name. I'll bet he names something 'Autumn Rose' everywhere he goes."

"And any one of those Autumn Roses may hold the key to finding the real Autumn Rose," said Madame Dragonfly.

"And your father," added Kirstin.

"Yes, him too," said Madame Dragonfly flatly.

They finished searching the house and then went home. Arthur and Dat turned on a soccer game, and Kirstin sat down at the computer to check her e-mail. She had three. Two were from her friends, but the third one had a blank where the sender's name should be, indicating that whoever sent it had intentionally removed that information. Also, it was encrypted, which added to the mystery. Encryption kept an e-mail secret by turning it into a code that was virtually impossible for anyone to break, except the person to whom the e-mail was sent. No one Kirstin knew would be sending her encrypted e-mail. She raised her eyebrows in surprise. "Do I open it?" she asked herself, moving the cursor to the "open" button and away from it in indecision. "Something funny is going on here." She was about to call Dat and Arthur, but she could hear them talking excitedly about the game, and she decided not to bother them. "Nothing much can happen to the computer just from opening an e-mail," she mumbled.

She took a deep breath and clicked it open. It said, "The next time you go riding, remember: U MARKS THE SPOT!" What does that mean? Kirstin wondered. Who sent it? Then she noticed something that made her forget these and the many other questions that were crowding into her head—an icon shaped like a bomb! And it was ticking! She watched in terror as the numbers counted down: "30 . . . 29 . . . 28 . . ."

CHAPTER 13

THE SECRET MAP

"A RTHUR!" yelled Kirstin as loud as she could. "There's a bomb on the computer!"

Arthur and Dat both came racing in. Arthur started looking at the hard drive tower, while Dat examined the printer and then the back of the monitor. In fact, they were looking at every part of the computer except the screen. "What are you doing?" Kirstin screamed in panic.

"You said there was a bomb on the computer," responded Arthur tensely. "We're looking for it! Where is it?"

"It's right there!" said Kirstin, pointing at the screen frantically. Meanwhile, the bomb counted down inexorably: "15 . . . 14 . . . 13 . . ."

Arthur stared at the screen for three precious seconds, thinking furiously. "Turn it off!" he said.

Kirstin reached for the power switch, but Dat stopped her. "No!" he said. "Bomb will explode! Bombs always built to explode when try to turn them off!" The bomb kept ticking, "7 . . . 6 . . . 5 . . ."

"What do I do?" asked Kirstin desperately.

"You're the computer genius!" said Arthur, staring at the screen helplessly. They all stood frozen as the final seconds counted down: "3 . . . 2 . . . 1. . . ." They all winced and tensed. The icon disappeared in a cartoon explosion with the word "BOOM!" in the middle. Then the e-mail Kirstin had been reading disappeared and the computer appeared to go back to normal.

Arthur blinked. "What happened?"

"I don't know," said Kirstin. She tried moving the mouse around and opening and running a few programs. Everything seemed to work. "Let me try running a system diagnostic," she said. The diagnostic checked the entire hard drive, but didn't find any problems. Kirstin didn't know what to try next, so she called her uncle Michael, who had forgotten more about computers than she knew. Arthur and Dat watched as she explained to him what had happened. Then she listened in silence while her uncle talked. "Huh!" she said. "I didn't know that." Then she listened some more while Arthur waited anxiously. Dat, who had figured out that there wasn't any physical danger for him to protect against, headed back into the family room to watch the rest of the soccer game. "OK," she said at last. "OK. . . . You're sure that's what happened? . . . Well, that's good news. Thanks, Uncle Michael! Tell Aunt Ruth hi from me!"

"Well?" said Arthur when she hung up the phone.

"Uncle Michael says that some encryption programs make the e-mail self-destruct one minute after it's opened," she explained. "That way no one can read it if they get into your computer. He says it sounds exactly like that's what happened." She looked at him a little sheepishly. "Sorry I freaked out on you guys like that."

"That's OK," said Arthur, breathing a sigh of relief. "So

everything's OK?" Kirstin nodded. "So what was the encrypted e-mail in the first place?"

Kirstin had been so rattled by the bomb that she had nearly forgotten about the mysterious e-mail. "Oh, yeah!" she said excitedly as she remembered. "I just got an encrypted e-mail from someone—I couldn't tell who—and it said that the next time I go riding, I should remember that 'U marks the spot.'"

"And that's what self-destructed?" asked Arthur.

"Yeah," said Kirstin. "Any idea what it means?"

Arthur shook his head. "I'll bet it's got something to do with Autumn Rose, though."

"Yeah, but what?"

"I don't know," said Arthur, "but the message said 'the next time you ride,' so maybe you have to be riding to find the U. Let's give Mrs. Armstrong a call to see if you can go riding tomorrow."

"Sounds good to me!" said Kirstin, who was always ready to go riding, whether a mystery was involved or not.

They called Mrs. Armstrong, who didn't have any openings the next day. They explained the situation to her, though, and she said that Kirstin could ride before they opened and look for the U that marked the spot. The lessons started at 8:30, so they would have to get there by 7:30 if they wanted time to conduct a thorough search. When Arthur heard that, he held back a groan. There seemed to be a conspiracy of horse people dedicated to waking him up way too early on summer mornings!

Arthur, Kirstin, and Dat drove into Autumn Rose's parking lot at 7:27 the next morning. Madame Dragonfly was busy that morning and was not able to join them. Kirstin eagerly scanned the landscape for anything that might look like a U. Dat watched alertly for possible attackers or spies, his hand hovering near the pistol he carried under his jacket. Arthur's attention was focused on the Egg McMuffin in his hand (he hadn't gotten up in time for breakfast) and on trying to keep from yawning too much.

All the horses were in their stables, so Kirstin had her choice of whom to take out riding. She was about to take Snowflake, a frisky white filly who loved to have fun, but she remembered that she was there to find clues, not have fun. She needed to take a slow, easy ride around Autumn Rose while she looked for the U. Snowflake would not want to take a slow, easy ride; she would want to run and jump and play, and that just wouldn't work today. "Next time, girl," said Kirstin as she walked past Snowflake's stall.

Kirstin decided to take out Jason, a gentle old brown gelding. He had been at Autumn Rose ever since Kirstin could remember, and he knew all the paths well. He would go at a slow, smooth walk and wouldn't try to leave the path, meaning that Kirstin could focus all her attention on her surroundings.

Kirstin got Jason saddled up and took him out. There were two paths she could take, the long winding one that went through the woods and the short one that went around the outside of the fenced pasture. Kirstin decided to take the long path. It held a lot more nooks and crannies where a secret sign could be hidden. Besides, she liked it better.

She squinted her eyes against the early morning sun as she rode across the pasture toward the trees. Maybe the message meant there were wildflowers planted in the shape of a U or a U-shaped mound or depression in the ground. But there didn't

seem to be any pattern to the clover and dandelions that speck-
led the grass with bright yellow and white, and she did not see
any shapes in the gently rolling pasture that looked at all like
the letter U.

A minute later, she was in the green shade of the trees, looking for an overgrown sign with a U on it, or maybe a U-shaped
tree branch. She didn't see any likely candidates, though. She
saw lots of Y's and I's, and even an H where someone had
nailed a board across two tree trunks, but no U's. Then she
had a brainstorm: Maybe the path made a U! She turned Jason
around, went back to the beginning of the forest (the path
across the pasture was straight and couldn't be a U), and re-
traced her steps, noting each twist and turn of the path. There
were plenty of curves in the path, but try as she might, she
couldn't find any that made a U.

She reached the end of the long path without any success,
so she started on the short one. Again, she had no luck. The
split-rail fence to her left ran around the pasture to make a
shape like a slightly squashed O, not a U. Nothing she saw in
the trees and thickets to her right looked like a U. She snapped
a twig off a dead tree branch and started using it to smack the
tops off tall grassy plants along the path. "Where can it be?"
she muttered as Jason walked peacefully along, completely
unconcerned by the frustrations of his rider.

Arthur was having no better luck back at the main building. He looked around for something that could be the U from
the exploding e-mail, but found nothing. After about twenty
minutes of fruitless searching, it occurred to him that Mrs.
Armstrong might know something. He tracked her down in
the stables, where she had just finished giving the horses their

morning oats. "Do you have any idea what this U could be?" he asked.

"I thought you might ask that," she said. She leaned against the stable doorpost and knitted her brows in thought. "I've been racking my old brains ever since Kirstin called last night and explained what had happened." She shook her head. "But I can't think of anything."

"Was there ever anything that people around here called the U?" Arthur asked. "A building maybe, or bend in the path? Was there ever a horse nicknamed U?"

She shook her head at each question. "I wish I could help you, but none of that rings a bell. If I think of anything, I'll let you know right away."

"Thanks," said Arthur. "Is there anyone else who might know more?"

"I thought of that too," she said with a smile. "The only one I can think of who would fit that bill is Jean-Luc, or Pierre, I guess."

"Hopefully I'll get a chance to ask him soon," said Arthur.

"I've been praying for him every day since he disappeared," she said with a look of concern.

"Yeah, me too," said Arthur. There wasn't anything more for him to do there, so he wandered out to find Kirstin. "I hope she's having better luck," he said to himself as he walked outside. He saw his sister coming around the last bend on the short path. It ended just outside the big brass-lettered "Autumn Rose" sign that arched over the main entrance. Arthur leaned against one of the signposts to wait for her. As she got closer, he could tell by the look on her face that she hadn't found anything. Also, she was energetically decapitating tall weeds with a stick as she rode past them. She had a habit of hitting inanimate objects when she was mad or frustrated, so that was a bad sign. "Find anything?" he asked as she rode up.

"Nothing," she said. She reached up and whacked the sign with her stick as she rode under it. Arthur looked up at the sign as she hit it. Then he stared. Then he hit himself in the head with his palm. "How could I have been so stupid?" he asked.

"Do you really want me to answer that?" said Kirstin with a mischievous grin.

Arthur ignored her. "Look!" he said. He pointed to the sign. All of the letters were made of brass, except one U was stainless steel. "How did we miss that? Quick, get a shovel!"

They got a shovel, and soon there was a big hole in the middle of the path leading up to the main building. A lot of the students and parents who walked by had odd looks for the sweaty young man who was so excitedly digging up the entrance to the horse farm. One woman even volunteered to call the police on her cell phone, but Mrs. Armstrong said not to bother and that everything was all right. She did make Arthur promise to fill up the hole and fix the path when he was done, though.

Arthur dug until noon, by which time the hole was over seven feet wide and five feet deep directly under the stainless steel U. Dat had been helping, but Arthur was still exhausted, and his arms were so sore that he could hardly move them. Despite his efforts, he hadn't found anything except some rocks, two rusty horseshoe nails, and lots and lots of dirt. "I don't understand," panted Arthur. "It's got to be here! It's just got to!"

"Have you tried looking under the U?" asked Kirstin.

Arthur looked at her like she'd lost her mind. "What do you think I've been doing this whole time?" he asked.

"No, I mean under the letter itself," explained Kirstin. "Have you tried taking it off the sign to see what's underneath?"

"No," said Arthur slowly. "No, I haven't." He nodded. "Great idea, Kirstin!" he said, his energy suddenly back. "Let's find a ladder and a screwdriver!"

Five minutes later, Arthur was flattening the bottom of the hole with the shovel so Mrs. Armstrong's stepladder could stand on it. Once that was done, he climbed to the top of the ladder (which was only about three feet above the edge of the hole) and reached up for the sign. He could barely get his hands high enough, and he struggled with the rusty screws that held the steel U in place. Kirstin, Dat, and Mrs. Armstrong waited eagerly at the bottom. Arthur's tortured arm and shoulder muscles burned with pain, but he didn't notice. One of the screws came out at last, then another, and finally the last screw was out! Arthur wiped drops of sweat out of his eyes and carefully lifted the metal letter away from the weathered wood.

A thin rectangular hole had been covered by the U. A folded piece of paper was in it! With trembling fingers, Arthur carefully took it out. It was yellow around the edges and looked brittle. He carefully descended the ladder and showed his find to the little crowd that waited at the bottom. Then he gently unfolded the paper, taking care to make sure it didn't crack at the folds. It was a hand-drawn map of an island with a big red X near the middle, and it was in Pierre LeGrand's handwriting!

CHAPTER 14

REALEMON

"This is so cool!" said Kirstin excitedly. "It must mean Mr. LeGrand is OK! He must have sent me the e-mail telling us where to find his map! I'll bet this is the same island in the picture at his house!"

"Yeah, I think you're right!" said Arthur. His brow furrowed as he looked at the map again. "But where is it?" No one had an answer for that question. They stared at the map in silence for several minutes, trying to unlock its secrets, but without success. Now that the excitement was over, Dat went back to his security guard duties, and Mrs. Armstrong left as well, saying that horse ranches get into trouble if left to themselves for too long.

Arthur and Kirstin still stood by the side of the main building, looking helplessly at the map. "I can't believe this!" fumed Kirstin in frustration. "We know where the treasure is on the island, but not where the island is on the world!"

They called Madame Dragonfly and gave her the good news that they had found the map and that her father appeared not to be in the hands of kidnappers after all, but also the bad news that they couldn't tell what the map actually showed. She was in a hurry, but she congratulated them for finding the map. Then she told them that she had hired detectives to solve mysteries, not bring them to her. She said she expected this one to be solved by the time they met for dinner that night, and then she hung up. "And how does she expect us to do that?" asked Arthur when they got off the phone.

Kirstin shrugged. "I don't know. She'd probably tell us to figure that out too."

Arthur chuckled ruefully. "That sounds just like something she'd say." He rolled his eyes and said, "Well, we'd better get started."

"How?" asked Kirstin.

Arthur tugged his lower lip. "Well, let's start with what we know." He started ticking points off on his fingers. "First, we know that Mr. LeGrand hid the map here. Second, no one else seems to have known about it, so he must have been the one who sent the e-mail to you. Third, the map by itself isn't enough to find the Autumn Rose, but fourth, the clues Mr. LeGrand gave us only told us how to find the map." He stopped and looked at the four fingers he was holding up, lost in thought.

"So what does that mean?" asked Kirstin.

Arthur sighed and sat down heavily on a wooden bench made out of a split log. "It means we're missing something, but what?"

Kirstin sat down beside her brother and thought for a minute. "It's probably something about the map. I mean, you're right, all the e-mail told us was how to find the map, so maybe that's all we need."

"But how can it be?" asked Arthur. He turned the map over, held it up to the sun, and looked at it sideways, trying to figure out its secrets.

They sat in silence for a while, both completely stumped. "Maybe he didn't write anything on the map because he didn't want anyone but himself to be able to use it," Kirstin said after a few minutes. Then she frowned and continued, "But if that were true, it wouldn't do us any good, and the e-mail doesn't make any sense."

"Maybe he told someone else too," said Arthur, "and he expects us to figure it out." He nodded as he thought the idea through. "I'll bet that's it. He's always been worried that someone would come looking for the Autumn Rose—someone he didn't want to find it. That's why he used a fake name, and that's why he buried it on an island. That's also why he made the map like this."

"And that's why he sent an encrypted e-mail and didn't tell us straight out where the map was," added Kirstin. "That makes sense. And even with all those precautions, he's still telling us as little as possible."

Arthur nodded. "He's also spreading the clues around so that it's hard for his enemies to find enough of them to be useful. But I'll bet I know within two guesses who we need to ask to get the last piece in the puzzle."

"I think you can rule out Madame Dragonfly," said Kirstin. "He hasn't talked to her since he disappeared, and that was before he hid the Autumn Rose or bought the horse ranch or anything."

Arthur arched his eyebrows. "How do you know that?"

"She told me," said Kirstin nonchalantly.

"Wow, you guys are practically best buddies compared to how she treats everybody else!" said Arthur. "OK, so we rule out your friend, Madame Dragonfly. That leaves Mrs.

Armstrong, but she didn't seem to know anything when we found the map."

"Maybe she doesn't know she knows, if you know what I mean," said Kirstin. "Maybe he didn't say to her, like, 'Here's how to use the secret map,' especially since she didn't know there was a secret map. Maybe we have to ask her the right questions.'"

"Sounds reasonable," said Arthur. "Let's go find her. You go ahead and ask 'the right questions,' and I'll jump in if I have anything to add." Kirstin didn't exactly know what the right questions were yet, but she hoped that if she asked enough questions, the right ones would come out. She just hoped she wouldn't look stupid in the process.

They found Mrs. Armstrong leaning on the fence by the corral, watching the lessons that were going on. "Tell her to sit up straighter," she commented to a teacher as he walked past. "That'll make it easier for her to keep her seat." She turned and saw Arthur and Kirstin walking up. "It's been quite an exciting day, hasn't it?" she remarked. "Any luck figuring out that map?"

"Actually, we were hoping you could help us with that," said Kirstin.

Mrs. Armstrong shook her head. "I already told you, he never said anything about that map to me. I never knew it was up there until today. By the way, have you put that dirt back yet, Arthur?"

Arthur winced. He had forgotten about that. "No, but I will before we leave," he promised.

"Just making sure," she said.

"Did Mr. LeGrand ever say *anything* to you?" asked Kirstin, trying to get back to the subject.

Mrs. Armstrong gave Kirstin an odd look. "He said lots of things," she said. "What are you getting at?"

"I mean, like, did he ever say anything about, you know, if anything ever happened to him?" Kirstin stammered lamely. *So much for not looking stupid,* she thought.

Mrs. Armstrong started to shake her head and opened her mouth to say something. Then she stopped and stood silent for a few seconds. "Wait here just a minute," she said. She hurried into the building. She came out again a few minutes later, holding something small in her hand. "Back when he put up that sign," she said as she walked over to them, "he gave me this." She held out an old yellow bottle cap that said "ReaLemon" on top. "He said that if anything ever happened to him, he wanted me to have this. I laughed, but he told me that it was a piece to a very valuable puzzle. He was very mysterious about it, so I figured it was a joke or something. It's been sitting on the bottom of my junk drawer for years and years. I'd completely forgotten about it."

"Thanks," said Arthur. He and Kirstin bent over the bottle cap, studying it closely.

"Well, I've got some paperwork to take care of," said Mrs. Armstrong as she turned back toward the building. "I'll be in the office if you need anything. Let me know when you're done with that cap." After she had gone about halfway to the door, she stopped and called back over her shoulder, "And don't forget about that hole!"

Arthur nodded and smiled, but was a little insulted that she felt she had to keep reminding him. He looked at the cap, slowly turning it over in his hands. "I don't get it," he said. "What does the cap to a bottle of lemon juice have to do with anything?"

"Lemon juice," repeated Kirstin thoughtfully.

"Yeah, what about it?" asked Arthur.

"You can use it for invisible ink," said Kirstin.

"Yeah, so?" said Arthur (he was tired and wasn't thinking very clearly). Then the lightbulb went on in his head and he said, "Oh, yeah! Let's find a lamp so we can heat the paper!" They ran inside and found a lamp. They took off the lampshade and Arthur held the map up to the lightbulb, moving it slowly back and forth so that the heat from the bulb would touch the entire piece of paper. As they watched breathlessly, brown writing appeared on the map! It said, "Autumn Rose is 20 meters west of red X," and a series of numbers appeared at the top of the map!

"Those must be the latitude and longitude of the island," said Arthur, pointing to the numbers. He saw the blank look on Kirstin's face. "You know, the lines that cut a globe up into squares? You'll learn about them in Geography. The longitude tells you how far east or west something is, and the latitude tells you how far north or south. If you've got the latitude and the longitude for a place, you can tell where it is anywhere in the world," he explained with a happy smile. It wasn't often that he knew something Kirstin didn't, so he was savoring the moment. "So knowing the latitude and longitude will tell us exactly where this island is."

"Come on," said Kirstin excitedly. "Let's go look it up on that map program at home!" They headed quickly out through the back of the building, which opened directly onto the parking lot. They got in the car and started home. Kirstin started to dial Madame Dragonfly's number on the cell phone, but Dat stopped her. "That's not digital. Scanners can pick it up, so whoever use one can hear everything you say. Wait 'til we get to your house to call, but please tell me what happen."

So they told Dat what had happened and showed him the bottle cap and the map. "Oops!" said Kirstin as she held up the bottle cap, "we forgot to return that!" Arthur winced and groaned. "It's not that bad," Kirstin said. "We'll just give it back to Mrs. Armstrong the next time we're out there."

"It *is* that bad!" lamented Arthur. "I just realized I'm going back out there as soon as I drop you guys off—I forgot to fill in that hole!"

CHAPTER 15

OFF TO THE ISLAND

While Arthur was back at the horse farm shoveling dirt, Kirstin was having some problems of her own. When she searched the map program for the latitude and longitude coordinates they had found, the computer screen didn't show any island at all, just empty blue water in Green Bay, between Wisconsin and Michigan. She tried running the same search on free Internet map programs, but they all showed the same thing. It was as if the island and its treasure had disappeared Atlantis-like beneath the gray waves of Lake Michigan.

This worried Kirstin; what if the coordinates were wrong? How would they find the island then? Then she realized that the island might be too small to show up on standard maps (except for sailor's charts, though this didn't occur to her). She searched the Internet and found a set of satellite photographs showing the entire United States. If it's really there, she thought, this will show it. She held her breath and waited nervously while the computer found the picture of those coordinates. The picture came up, and there was the island! "Yes!" she said and let out her breath in relief. She printed the picture and called Madame Dragonfly to let her know that they had found the island. "Of course you did," said Madame Dragonfly. "Tell me the details over dinner. Oh, and make sure to pack. We'll be leaving tomorrow morning to go up to this island. Tell Dat to make the arrangements."

"How did you know?" asked Kirstin.

"Know what?" asked Madame Dragonfly.

"How did you know that we would find the island? It sure wasn't easy!"

Madame Dragonfly paused for a few seconds. "I have seen you and your brother perform, and I have faith in you, sometimes even more faith than you have in yourselves. Now I have to go. I'm sorry, but I have a conference call in three minutes, and I don't really have time to talk right now. Good-bye." She hung up, and so did Kirstin, who was feeling about ten feet tall. She could tell that Madame Dragonfly gave out compliments about as often as it snowed in Dallas.

She relayed the news to Dat, who immediately got on the phone to make travel arrangements. Then she ran upstairs to pack. She pulled out her suitcase, then realized she couldn't use it. Her mother had bought it for her when she was nine, and it had cutesy horses on it. It was fine for a nine year old, and even today it was OK for trips where only her family would see it, but she simply *couldn't* take it on a detective trip with someone like Madame Dragonfly.

Just then, Arthur came trudging slowly up the stairs. "Hey Arthur," she said, going out to meet him in the hallway. Then she got a whiff of him. "Pee-yew!" she said, backing up and waving her hand in front of her face. "You stink! Can I borrow one of your suitcases?"

He arched his eyebrows, then gave her a pouty, sad look. "I don't know if I can let you after you hurt my feelings like that.

Give me a hug and maybe I'll feel better." He reached out his dirty, smelly arms and started walking toward her.

"Aaak! No, Arthur!" she screamed. "Get away from me!" She turned, ran into her room, and locked the door. "Can I *please* have your suitcase?" she pleaded as soon as she was safe.

Once Arthur stopped laughing, he said, "Why? Where are you going?"

"Oh, I forgot to tell you," Kirstin answered from behind the door. "We're going to the island. It's in Green Bay, just north of Wisconsin, in Door County. Dat's making the travel arrangements right now, and we're supposed to be ready to leave tomorrow morning."

"Wow!" said Arthur. "Madame Dragonfly doesn't waste any time, does she? You can probably borrow one of my suitcases. I'll check and let you know after I take a shower."

"Thanks. And we'll need to talk to Mom and Dad too," replied Kirstin.

"Oh, yeah," said Arthur. He thought for a moment. That would take some diplomacy and negotiating skill. "Let me handle this. I'll talk to Dad after I get cleaned up."

The whole time he was in the shower, Arthur rehearsed his arguments for why they should be allowed to go to Door County. He felt pretty good about them by the time he got dressed. Then he went over them with Kirstin, who added a few suggestions.

Now it was show time. He took a deep breath and walked nonchalantly into the den, where their father was working. "Hi, Dad," he said casually.

His dad glanced up over his glasses, took a quick look at Arthur, and turned back to the computer screen. "Hi, Arthur. No."

Arthur was stunned. "But . . . but . . . I was just, uh," he stammered. What would he tell Kirstin? Worse, what would he tell Madame Dragonfly? That was *not* a conversation he wanted to have.

His dad looked up at him again and chuckled. "Sorry, I couldn't resist. Your I'm-going-to-ask-for-something look is a little too obvious. What can I do for you?"

Arthur took a breath and tried to settle his jangled nerves. "Well, it's not really something I want you to do for me. It's more that we would like you to let us do something. You know how you're going to Washington, D.C., for that conference this weekend?"

"I seem to remember something about that," his dad commented with a wry smile and a glance at the packed garment bag beside his desk.

"OK, well, Madame Dragonfly is going to Door County tomorrow morning to try to find the Autumn Rose, and she's taking Dat with her, so we thought it would probably be a good idea if we went with them." His dad looked skeptical, so Arthur hurried on. "I mean, it wouldn't be that safe for us to stay with Aunt Mary or go with you guys, would it? Without Dat, there wouldn't be anything to keep the bad guys from getting us. And if we go to Door County, we'll have Vladimir and Dat *both* to protect us. So really, the safest and most responsible thing we can do is go to Door County with them."

Mr. Davis didn't answer right away. He drummed his fingers on the desk and looked out the window as Arthur stood waiting nervously. "I'm not sure," he said. "Don't you think that's pretty risky?"

Arthur had thought out an answer for this and gave it

smoothly. "Maybe, but the risk of going with them is a lot less than the risk of staying here. After all, up there we'll have two trained bodyguards watching us night and day, but here the best the police can offer is to have one squad car parked outside our house when they can spare it."

"Maybe," his dad said thoughtfully, "maybe. But maybe the best thing would be for us to take you to D.C. with us or cancel our trip."

"But how will that solve the problem?" countered Arthur. "No offense, but how can you guys protect us? I mean, you don't even own a gun."

Mr. Davis thought some more. "I'll talk to your mother, and we'll think about it. This isn't exactly like you're asking to go on a camping trip with your friends."

Arthur waited nervously while his parents discussed the matter in the kitchen with the door closed. At first, he sat in the den and tried to read a magazine, but he couldn't concentrate as the minutes slowly ticked by. After about twenty minutes, he had only gotten through one page of the article he was reading, and he couldn't remember what it said. He gave up on the magazine and went upstairs to pack, hoping he would get the answer he wanted. He was just deciding how many pairs of underwear he would need when he heard the kitchen door open.

Arthur was already halfway down the stairs when Mr. Davis called him and Kirstin. Once they were all seated around the kitchen table, Mr. Davis said, "Everything in this case has turned out to be much more dangerous than we thought, and there's no reason to think this trip to Door County will be any exception." Arthur started to object, but his dad held up his hand. "But you're probably right that staying here or coming to D.C. with us would be at least as dangerous. There are really no good options, but letting you go to Door County is the least bad." Kirstin and Arthur both nodded in agreement.

"But be careful," urged Mrs. Davis. "Call us if you get in any trouble. And pray about what you're doing, even if it doesn't look like there'll be any trouble." She scribbled a phone number on a piece of paper and handed it to Arthur. "Here's the hotel we'll be at."

"We will, Mom," said Kirstin. "Pray for us too, OK?"

Mrs. Davis smiled and patted Kirstin's hand. "We always do."

Two hours later, Arthur and Kirstin were both packed (and both using Arthur's suitcases) and waiting in the hotel lobby for Madame Dragonfly. Dat was with them, of course, pacing back and forth across the marble floor and watching for anyone or anything suspicious. Madame Dragonfly and Vladimir finally came down ten minutes late, and they all sat down to dinner in the hotel's restaurant. Arthur and Kirstin gave their reports of the day's activities. Then it was Dat's turn. He talked about the airlines he had contacted and the great hotel he had found in Sister Bay, Wisconsin, the closest town to the island, but never actually said how they would be getting there. Also, he fidgeted nervously with his dessert fork while he was talking and didn't look Madame Dragonfly in the eye. She, of course, noticed this immediately and stopped him after less than two minutes. "So when does our flight leave?" she asked.

"There are no flights that actually go there," he said. "We

have to go to Sturgeon Bay, then drive half hour to Sister Bay, but that flight takes long time and has many stopovers."

"So you chartered a plane," said Madame Dragonfly, pinning him with her sharp eyes.

Dat squirmed uncomfortably. "No. I didn't do that either," he said. "I think if we do that, we have to file flight plan, tell people at airport where we are going, and maybe someone find out and get there before us. I think maybe best plan is to drive." His English and his accent got worse when he was nervous, so Arthur and Kirstin had to struggle to understand everything he said.

"You know I hate long car trips," said Madame Dragonfly with a frown.

"I know," said Dat miserably, "but it seemed best plan."

Madame Dragonfly thought for a moment. "Very well," she said. "I suppose you're right." Dat's face relaxed and he sat back in his chair. "We'll take two cars. I'll take one. You and Vladimir take the other." She waved off his suggestion that one of the bodyguards drive each car. "I get nauseous if I'm not driving," she said. "Besides, you both smoke, and I hate being in a car full of cigarette smoke."

They decided to take different routes to throw off any pursuers. They hoped that their enemies wouldn't be able to follow both cars at the same time and at least one of them would get to their destination unwatched.

Arthur and Kirstin had their choice of riding with Madame Dragonfly or her bodyguards. For Kirstin, the choice was easy. She liked Madame Dragonfly, she hated cigarette smoke, and she was sure she'd be bored to death by the conversation in Vladimir and Dat's car. Arthur, however, had a tough decision to make. He didn't much like the idea of spending five and a half hours (which was about how long the trip north to Sister Bay would take) in a car with two smokers, but he also didn't want to spend that much time with Madame Dragonfly. He always felt like he was walking on egg shells around her, and he could never really relax. Dat, on the other hand, was a lot easier to spend time with, even if he did smoke. Arthur ultimately decided that he would ride with the two men and just keep the window rolled down.

The two cars pulled out of the Davises' driveway at seven the next morning. Madame Dragonfly and Kirstin sat together in the front seat of the first car, chatting about the trip. Vladimir and Dat sat in the front seat of the second car, talking about last night's soccer game, while Arthur lay in the backseat with his eyes shut, trying to go back to sleep.

Arthur was stiff and sore from all the hard work he had done at the horse farm the day before. As he struggled to find a position where nothing hurt, he comforted himself with the thought that at least the hard part of solving this mystery was over. He was very, very wrong about that, but at least thinking it helped him go to sleep.

CHAPTER 16

WHAT HAPPENED AT A LONELY WAYSIDE

Arthur slept fitfully in the backseat for over two hours as they drove through the northern suburbs of Chicago, the southern suburbs of Milwaukee, the city of Milwaukee, and then the northern suburbs of Milwaukee.

By the time Arthur opened his eyes again, they had at last left all the built-up areas and the traffic jams that went with them behind. They were driving through the farm country and thick forests of eastern Wisconsin. Arthur didn't know this, though, because he was still lying on his back, so all he could see through the windows was the cloudy sky above them. He tried to sit up, but every single muscle in his body was suddenly on fire, or at least that's the way it felt. He groaned and lay back down. Dat turned and gave Arthur a smile that was half-amused and half-sympathetic. "I think you are a little sore from yesterday," he observed. Arthur nodded with a wince. "Sleeping all morning in car only makes it worse," continued Dat, shaking his head. "We are stopping at a wayside soon. You can stretch out some there."

"Thanks," moaned Arthur.

Five minutes later, they pulled into a lonely rest area cut

from the surrounding cornfields. The bathrooms and the little information booth were the only buildings for miles around. "You coming?" asked Dat as he and Vladimir opened their doors.

"I'll be there in a minute," said Arthur as he painfully began unbending his stiff limbs and massaging the kinks out of his legs.

"OK," said Dat and got out. Left alone in the car, Arthur leaned back into a more comfortable position. His legs felt better after he had worked on them, so he started kneading his arms as well.

Arthur was just getting ready to get out of the car when he heard a strangled scream! He crouched down behind the front seat and carefully peered out at what was happening. Three large Asian men in jeans and T-shirts and with black gloves on their hands were carrying a struggling Vladimir out of the bathroom. His mouth, arms, and legs were bound with silver duct tape. A few seconds later, two more men (also wearing jeans, T-shirts, and gloves) came out dragging Dat's limp body. He also was bound with duct tape. The men carried Dat and Vladimir around to the other side of the building.

No one else appeared. There was a clump of bushes at the edge of the bathrooms. Beyond that was a sidewalk, and then another parking lot on the other side of the buildings. His heart racing, Arthur felt for his cell phone. With a sinking feeling, he realized that he had left it at home.

He picked up his casebook, got out of the car, and ran as fast as he could to the bushes. He hid behind them and jotted down quick descriptions of the cars and license plate numbers in the casebook: "Gray—X139U8 (IL); White—EM4239

(IL)." He saw two men loading Dat into the white car. Vladimir was still struggling, but they poured some liquid onto a cloth and put the cloth over his face. After a few seconds, he went limp, and they put him in the gray car.

Arthur started writing down descriptions of the men, but stopped when it occurred to him that he had seen five, not four. *Where did that fifth guy go?* he wondered. He looked around the parking lot, but didn't see him anywhere. Then he heard a car door slam behind him!

Arthur turned as quietly and quickly as he could, just in time to hear the engine start and see the car he had been riding in begin to move. His heart sank as he watched the car drive out of the parking lot, but it drove back into the second parking lot and stopped near the two other cars. The man who was driving it got out, and he and another member of the jeans-and-T-shirt gang (which was how Arthur was beginning to think of them) began going through the car methodically but quickly. They didn't seem to be finding what they were looking for, and they began to act frustrated; they were snapping at each other and banging their fists into their palms. *I wonder what they're looking for,* thought Arthur. Then he realized that both the map and the directions to their hotel in Sister Bay were in his casebook—and nowhere else. "They don't know where we're going!" Arthur whispered quietly to himself. "And they're looking for directions!"

The men were finished looking through the car. One of them went over to the gray car and stood by the passenger side door. Someone inside rolled down the window, but Arthur couldn't see who it was. The man outside the car was standing very straight, unnaturally straight in fact. *Exactly like a soldier stands when he's talking to a superior officer,* thought Arthur. He wrote that down in his book too.

The man walked away from the car, and Arthur got a good look at the person he had been talking to. It was an old Asian man with a crewcut, a square face, and thick black hair. Unfortunately, the man in the car also got a good look at Arthur! He pointed straight at Arthur and started yelling in a foreign language.

Arthur turned and ran. As he crossed the parking lot at top speed, he could hear squealing tires and running feet behind him. He saw a field of corn straight ahead across the highway. It was almost ready for harvest and stood taller than his head. *If I can just reach the corn,* thought Arthur as he ran, *maybe I can hide.*

Arthur snuck a look over his shoulder. The gray car was too far away to cut him off, but two members of the jeans-and-T-shirt gang were gaining on him. Even though he was one of the fastest members of his soccer team and had a twenty yard head start, Arthur wasn't sure he would make it to the corn in time. He crossed the highway, scrambled down the embankment, and splashed across a drainage ditch. He could hear, but dared not look to see, his pursuers coming down the embankment. He raced across the dirt road at the edge of the field and plunged into the corn!

Ears of corn slapped Arthur painfully in the face and arms as he ran, sprinting down one row, then cutting across two or three rows and sprinting down another. He could hear the two men crashing through the corn behind him and yelling to each other. As he ran, Arthur realized that he faced a dilemma: If he kept moving, the men could follow the noise he made, but if he stopped, they would know more or less where he was from where the noise stopped and they would soon find him. Either way, he would probably get caught.

Arthur suddenly found himself at the edge of the field. He looked desperately from left to right. He spotted a big corrugated steel pipe that allowed drainage water to flow under the highway. He immediately ducked into it and crawled as fast as he could through the dark, cold water. He hardly noticed the painful bruises and scrapes he was getting on his hands and knees from the rough metal of the pipe. All he cared about was reaching the circle of light at the other end of it.

He reached the end of the pipe and splashed across a stream that flowed on the other side. The banks of the stream were covered with thick, tall grass. Arthur pulled himself out of the water, crawled a few feet into the grass, and lay down, exhausted. As he lay there, he silently but fervently prayed that they wouldn't catch him. He heard men's voices talking in a foreign language, but they were far away and didn't seem to be getting any closer. To his relief, he did not hear any splashing in the stream.

Arthur lay perfectly still, breathing as quietly as possible. A big ant crawled across his leg and a sharp stick was poking him painfully in the back, but he didn't move. The voices stopped, but he still didn't move. The only sounds were made by a light wind blowing through the grass and occasional cars and trucks driving by on the highway. A frog began to croak by the water on the other side of the stream. He heard a jet plane fly over, but couldn't see it because of the low ceiling of thick gray clouds that covered the sky. *It looks like it might rain,* thought Arthur as he lay in the grass. A few seconds later, heavy drops began to fall on his face.

A minute later, the downpour began in earnest. Then Arthur carefully got up. He was already soaking wet, so the rain did not bother him. He thought it might bother the jeans-and-T-shirt gang, however, and might make them stop looking for him, if they hadn't already. Also, the rain would make it harder for anyone driving by on the highway (such as the gang in their gray and white cars) to see him. Arthur made his way back to the rest area, keeping to cover as much as he could and staying a stone's throw away from the highway.

After half an hour of creeping through thorny thickets and crawling through wet grass, Arthur crouched behind a clump of weeds, looking out over the rest area. There were no cars in either parking lot, and no people either. The place looked completely deserted. Still, it was possible that they were setting a trap for him. He crept carefully around the outer edge of the rest area clearing, looking for anyone who might be waiting in ambush for him.

Once he was sure it was safe, Arthur walked down into the parking lot. There was no trace of the gang anywhere. Arthur suddenly realized that there was no trace of his car either, and his heart sank. He was completely alone in the middle of nowhere with no car. He checked his wallet and found that he also had no money. All he had with him was his soggy casebook, which he had somehow kept from dropping during the chase. Dat and Vladimir had been caught by a well-organized gang, and Arthur had only barely escaped. Now the same gang that had so easily caught Madame Dragonfly's expert bodyguards was going after her and Kirstin. The men who had ambushed them probably didn't know where to go, but they had Dat and Vladimir now. Arthur knew that Madame Dragonfly's guards would never willingly betray her or the Davises, but he also knew that there were drugs that could force information out of even the toughest men.

Arthur stood in the middle of the parking lot feeling very alone and helpless. There was no phone in the rest area he could use to call for help, he had no car to drive to get help, and powerful enemies were closing in on his sister and Madame Dragonfly. He had not cried since he was eight years old, not even when he broke his leg during a game and had to be carried off on a stretcher, but he was very close to crying now.

CHAPTER 17

STUCK

Arthur said a prayer asking God to watch over Kirstin and Madame Dragonfly and deliver Dat and Vladimir from their enemies, and that made him feel a little better. The rain stopped while he was praying, and that made him feel better still. Then a car pulled into the parking lot, and his heart jumped for joy.

Arthur ran toward the car, yelling and waving his arms. The passenger door opened, and an elderly woman started to get out. When she saw Arthur running toward her, she screamed and yelled, "Harold, start the car! Start the car!" She slammed her door, and the tires squealed as the car backed up at full speed.

"No, wait!" shouted Arthur. He reached the car and yelled, "Please wait!" at the driver, an old man in a golf hat, presumably named Harold. But the old man ignored Arthur's pleas, and Arthur had to jump back to avoid getting run over. The car sped out of the parking lot, knocking down a sign on the way out, and raced away.

As he watched Harold and his wife drive away, Arthur mentally kicked himself. He realized that he must have looked like a wild maniac. He was soaking wet, his clothing was torn and dirty, and he had run at them screaming and waving his arms. Of course he had scared them off! He should have waited until they were out of their car. Then he should have walked over calmly and asked them for help.

He picked up a rock and threw it as hard as he could in frustration. He scowled as he watched the rock sail through the air and disappear into the bushes on the far side of the lot. Then his scowl turned into a look of surprise. The rock had not landed with the soft "thunk" he had expected. Instead, it had made a hard "bonk," as if it had hit something made of metal. Arthur looked more carefully at the bushes and saw that something big appeared to be hidden behind them. He jogged over for a closer look. He pushed the bushes aside, then yelled, "Yes!" and pumped his fist in the air. His car was there, completely undamaged except for a brand new dent in the roof where the rock had landed!

He looked through the window and saw the keys still in the ignition. *Great!* he thought. *They just hid the car and left it!* He tried the door, but it was locked. Oh well, he couldn't ask for everything.

Arthur walked back to the parking lot with the idea of finding a wire or piece of sheet metal to use to pick the lock on his car door. If he didn't find one, he would get a big rock and smash in the car door window. He did not like the idea of smashing the window on his mother's car, particularly after he had just dented the roof, but he really wouldn't have much choice. He had to get someplace where he could call the police and warn Kirstin and Madame Dragonfly, and he had to do it *fast*.

Arthur didn't need to worry about the car door, because when he got back to the parking lot the police were there waiting for him. He was delighted to see them, of course, but he remembered his experience with Harold and his wife, so he didn't yell and run toward them. It's a good thing he didn't, because he might have gotten shot if he did. As soon as the police saw him, they yelled "Freeze!" and pointed their guns at him. Arthur froze.

One of the policemen pointing a gun at Arthur yelled, "Hands in the air!" Arthur put his hands up as another officer ran over to him. He frisked Arthur, pulled Arthur's wallet out of his pocket and grabbed the casebook, then handcuffed him. "What's going on?" demanded Arthur indignantly.

"You're under arrest for assault, intimidation, and reckless endangerment . . . Mr. Davis," said the policeman as he stepped back and glanced at Arthur's driver's license. "Now move!" He pushed Arthur in the direction of the police car.

"What?!" said Arthur in amazement. He stopped and looked back at the second policeman in shock.

"Keep moving!" barked the first policeman, who was still pointing a gun at Arthur's chest. "You have the right to remain silent. Anything you say can and will be used against you in a court of law. You have the right to an attorney. . . ."

Arthur stumbled forward in a daze, not really listening to the *Miranda* warnings the policeman was giving him. Harold must have called the police, Arthur realized. They were here to arrest the wild man who had frightened the old couple. "Wait," he said as they pushed him into the car, "this is all a big misunderstanding!"

"Yeah, yeah, yeah," said the first policeman, who looked like he had heard that before. He was the older of the two officers and seemed to be in charge.

"No really," insisted Arthur from inside the squad car. "I was stuck here, and I needed help, so I ran over to this old couple when they pulled in. I must have scared them by accident, because they slammed their doors and drove away really fast. They knocked down that sign as they drove away." He gestured with his head toward the broken signpost.

"So how did you get stuck?" asked the first policeman skeptically.

Arthur hesitated for a moment. The easy thing to do would be to lie, of course. He could say that he just drove off the side of the parking lot and then locked his keys in the car by mistake. The police might believe that and let him go. They almost certainly wouldn't believe the truth, and they would probably think he was either crazy or hiding something. Arthur had never lied to the police, though, and he wasn't going to start now.

"I know this is going to sound unbelievable," he began, and he told the policemen what had happened at the rest area and enough of the background so that it made sense. He said "sir" a lot and did his best to make a good impression on the officers. He also pointed out that most of his story was corroborated by the soggy casebook in the policeman's hand and that he would not have had time to write down everything in the casebook in the time between his encounter with Mr. and Mrs. Harold and his arrest. The officer thumbed through the casebook and took notes as Arthur talked.

"Mind if we look through your car?" asked the older policeman. Arthur said of course he didn't mind, and the younger officer left to go search his car.

"So why did they leave your car here with the keys in the

ignition?" asked the older policeman when Arthur finished his story. "Why not at least slash the tires or throw the keys in the canal?"

"I've been thinking about that," said Arthur. "The only explanation I can think of is that they don't want to leave any evidence that would back up my story. They knew I'd call the cops, but they didn't want you to believe me. They wanted to make it look like I was either crazy or making up dumb lies to cover up the fact that I drove my mom's car into the bushes and then locked the keys inside. The longer they can keep you guys from getting involved, the better off they are."

"Uh-huh," said the policeman thoughtfully. He looked undecided as to whether to believe Arthur or not. Then the younger policeman walked up and muttered something in the first policeman's ear. The older officer's face hardened. "Son, do you use any controlled substances?" he asked.

"What?" asked Arthur, confused.

"Drugs, son. Do you use drugs?" asked the first policeman.

"No, sir!" insisted Arthur vehemently.

"Then what's this?" asked the second policeman accusingly as he held up a plastic bag containing white powder.

"I don't know," said Arthur honestly.

"It was in the glove compartment of your car," said the younger policeman flatly.

"It's all part of the setup!" Arthur insisted desperately. As soon as the words were out of his mouth, he knew that he sounded like a paranoid drug addict. The looks on the faces of both policemen made it clear that they thought the same thing.

"If it was on the car seat, I might believe you," said the older policeman. "But why would they put it in your glove compartment where no one would see it while they were jimmying your lock?"

"They . . . they must have realized that the first thing you'd do when you got the door open would be ask for proof that it was my car," said Arthur, thinking quickly. "I'd open the glove compartment to get out the certificate of title, and you'd see it then!"

"Maybe," said the older policeman, "maybe. For right now, though, we're going to have to take you in. We'll send a tow truck to take your car to the impound lot."

Arthur threw his head against the back of his seat in frustration. "Will you at least call and warn Madame Dragonfly and my sister?" he asked. "And could you put out an APB on those two cars?"

"Do you remember the license plate numbers?" asked the older policeman.

"I thought I told you they were written down in my casebook," said Arthur a little rudely. So many bad things had happened to him so fast that his manners were beginning to fray.

The policeman didn't get mad, however. He held up the casebook, which was open to the last page. The ink on that page had run badly, and the license plate numbers were illegible. Arthur closed his eyes and flopped back in his seat. "I can't believe this is happening," he said weakly.

"We'll call the Sister Bay police and ask them to look in on your friends," said the policeman, with a sympathetic tone in his voice. "We've already left a message for this Officer MacGregor, but he wasn't there. I'll personally try again when we get back to the station and see if we can check out your story. I'm afraid you're going to have to spend at least tonight with us, though. We can't just ignore the drugs in your car, for one thing."

Arthur nodded listlessly, his eyes still shut. "I understand." He had no idea what to do next. He felt in his pockets for the piece of paper with the number of his parents' hotel. He found it, but it was now a completely unreadable lump of wet paper glop. *Great, just great.*

He couldn't call his parents, Officer MacGregor wasn't in, and the police were already going to get in contact with Kirstin and Madame Dragonfly, if they could reach them in time. Was there anyone else he should try to call? He wondered about that for a minute, then he sat up and opened his eyes. "Say, do I get to make a phone call?"

"Yeah sure, kid," said the policeman.

"Is it OK if it's long distance?" asked Arthur.

"No problem," said the policeman. "Just keep it short."

"OK," agreed Arthur. The drive back to the police station seemed to take forever, and Arthur fidgeted impatiently the whole way. Many precious minutes slipped by as they drove through fields of corn and soybeans, little country towns, and glades of trees. It was late afternoon by now, and the sun hung low in the western sky, its lazy golden light making all the colors of the landscape warm and rich. The drive was actually very pretty, but of course Arthur was in no mood to enjoy it.

At last they reached the police station. Arthur immediately asked if he could make his phone call. No, he was told, he would have to wait until they were done processing him. They took his fingerprints and picture, had him fill out forms, and asked him questions, most of which he had already answered for the officers who had arrested him. Finally, they let him use the phone. He needed his casebook for the number, though, and had to argue with them for almost ten minutes before they reluctantly allowed him to look at it long enough to find and dial the number (which he had fortunately written in pencil, so it was still legible).

Arthur listened impatiently as the phone rang and rang at the other end. "Please be there! Please be there!" he whispered fervently. With all that had been going wrong, he more than half expected that no one would answer.

After twelve rings, a sleepy man's voice answered. "Allo, allo?" it said.

"Mr. Nguyen!" said Arthur, relief flooding through him. "Something terrible has happened! Actually, a bunch of terrible things have happened!"

"Tell me," said Mr. Nguyen's voice, now crisp and very much awake.

CHAPTER 18

THIOPENTAL SODIUM

The first thing Dat noticed when he began to regain consciousness was that someone was slapping him. He groggily tried to put up his hands to ward off the blows, but he couldn't. "Enough! He is awake," a familiar voice said in Vietnamese. Immediately the slapping stopped.

Dat opened his eyes in a squint. All he could see was a very bright light pointed at his face. Other than that, the room was completely dark. Dat tried to get up, but found that his hands and feet were tied to the chair in which he found himself sitting. He was confused for an instant. Then he remembered what had happened at the wayside. "Where is the Autumn Rose?" asked the voice. Dat said nothing. *Where had he heard that voice before?* he wondered. "Where is the Autumn Rose?" the voice repeated. Again, Dat sat stubbornly silent.

"Doctor, give him thiopental sodium," said the familiar voice. Dat steeled himself. Thiopental sodium was a drug often used in interrogations in Vietnam because it confused prisoners and made it hard for them to lie.

A pudgy white man holding a syringe walked up to Dat. "Dr. Ivanov!" exclaimed Dat. Dr. Ivanov worked with the Vietnamese military intelligence units, or at least he had when Dat was in the Vietnamese army. Dat had been a guard at the intelligence headquarters and had often seen Dr. Ivanov go in carrying his black bag of drugs to help with an interrogation. Dat shuddered as he remembered the vacant stares of the prisoners that came out afterward and, even worse, the ones that had to be rushed to the hospital because they had been given an overdose of drugs. Dr. Ivanov was almost as ruthless as the man he worked for, General Tran, who—Dat felt the hair rise on the back of his neck as he remembered—*whose voice was the one he had just heard!* "General Tran, what are you doing here?" asked Dat, as Dr. Ivanov injected the thiopental sodium into his arm.

The voice chuckled. "I'll be asking the questions here, Corporal Le." No one said anything for a while as they waited for the drug to take effect. Dat felt his mind becoming cloudy and desperately fought to keep focused. *Focused on what?* he asked himself, and he had to fumble for the answer.

The doctor walked over to Dat again and checked his pupils, pulse, and breathing. "Go ahead," he said. "He's ready."

"Where is the Autumn Rose?" repeated General Tran for a third time. Dat felt an immediate urge to answer, but he resisted as hard as he could, even though he wasn't exactly sure why. He shook his head and said nothing. "Why are you shaking your head?" asked the general.

"I . . . I can't say anything," said Dat.

"Why not?" asked the general.

Dat pondered for several seconds. It would be such a relief to just let it out, but he knew he shouldn't. "Because it's a secret," he said at last.

"Did your commanding officer tell you it was secret?"

Dat didn't recall his commanding officer saying anything. "No."

"Then who did?"

Dat couldn't recall clearly. "I don't remember," he said.

"Did *anyone* ever actually tell you it was a secret?"

"No," Dat said slowly, "no, but—"

"Then tell me where it is," said the general insistently.

"I can't," said Dat with effort. It was so hard to keep holding it back.

"Soldier, are you being insubordinate?" snapped the general.

"No, sir!" said Dat reflexively. Was he still a soldier? He couldn't quite remember.

"You tell me, Corporal!" commanded the general. "And that's a direct order!"

"I'm sorry, sir," said Dat after a moment. "What was the question?"

"Where is the Autumn Rose?" asked the general, almost shouting.

Dat remembered something about a map and an island, but couldn't get it all to make sense in his head. "I don't know, sir," he said.

General Tran muttered something unpleasant under his breath. "Then where were you going?"

Dat hesitated. For some reason, he felt that he shouldn't tell the general. He couldn't quite remember why, though. "Answer the question, Corporal!" ordered General Tran.

"The White Fish Inn, sir!" said Dat reflexively.

"And where is that?"

"I don't remember, sir. Arthur had the directions," said Dat. At the mention of Arthur's name, he realized that he had made a mistake. "Please, sir, don't tell him I told you," he pleaded, but the general was not listening. He was giving orders to his men to find the White Fish Inn, and find it fast.

CHAPTER 19

MADAME DRAGONFLY'S MEMORIES

The biggest problem that Madame Dragonfly and Kirstin had on their trip to the White Fish Inn was deciding where to stop for lunch. They had to find a place that was fast enough to get them back on the road in half an hour (Madame wanted to be in Sister Bay as soon as possible), but served something other than "that greasy American fast food," as Madame Dragonfly put it with a look of distaste. They ultimately couldn't find anything, so they stopped at a grocery store and bought fruit, cheese, and mineral water.

The car grew awkwardly silent after they finished eating, so Kirstin decided to start a conversation. "So, what does the Autumn Rose look like?"

Madame Dragonfly sighed. "It's the most beautiful thing I have ever seen," she said. "It's a black pearl as big as your fist." She balled her right hand into a fist and held it up. Kirstin made a fist too, and noticed that hers was actually bigger than Madame Dragonfly's. "It's perfectly round without the slightest flaw," she continued. "It's completely black when you look at it indoors, but if you look at it in the sun, it has a sheen, an iridescence, like the hint of a rainbow. And if you hold it in front of the sun, you see a most beautiful glow of gold and pink and red all around its edge. A poet who saw it centuries ago said that it was like light from heaven let in through a crack in the world."

Kirstin looked over at Madame Dragonfly and almost didn't recognize her. Her face wore a gentle, wistful smile and her eyes shone with unshed tears. The pearl sounded lovely to Kirstin, but she would never have guessed that anything could have this effect on Madame Dragonfly. She acted almost as if she was talking about someone she loved deeply. "Does it remind you of your father?" asked Kirstin.

Madame Dragonfly sniffed and blinked away her tears. "No," she said. "It reminds me of . . ." She knit her brows and glanced over at Kirstin. "It's funny you should bring that up. The Autumn Rose has always reminded me of something, but I could never remember what. When I was a girl, I would stare at it until my eyes ached. I can even see it now in my mind's eye, but I've never been able to figure out what it reminds me of."

"It sounds really incredibly beautiful," said Kirstin. "Your father must have loved you a lot to give it to you."

"He didn't give it to me, remember?" replied Madame Dragonfly with a wry smile. "That's why we're on this trip. He just promised that he would give it to me when I was ready." She paused. "But I see what you mean. He promised me the greatest treasure he ever possessed, so he must love me. But then he abandoned my mother and me less than a week later and I never heard from him again."

"He must have had a good reason," said Kirstin. She didn't want to think that the nice old man she had met would have disappeared from his daughter's and wife's lives voluntarily.

"If he did, he never told it to me," said Madame Dragonfly with a slight edge to her voice.

"What was your mother like?" asked Kirstin to change the subject.

"My mother? I remember a man once describing her as a Vietnamese Audrey Hepburn with the soul of Machiavelli, which he meant as a compliment." She glanced over at Kirstin, whose blank look showed that she didn't know what this meant. "She was beautiful and elegant, and she had an incredible ability to understand what was going on between people and make them do what she wanted. She was always looking out for me and protecting me, and she was very good at it. She was a terrible enemy, but a wonderful friend. Even today, when I am faced with a problem, I often ask myself what she would do." She fell silent for a moment as she wandered among her memories. "Ah, Kirstin, you are reminding me of things I have not thought of in a very long time."

"Was your father the same way?" asked Kirstin.

"Oh, yes, at least when he was young. Have you heard how he and my mother met?" Kirstin shook her head. "She was a fashionable young woman from a well-to-do family living in an expensive apartment in Saigon."

"Did she have a job?" asked Kirstin.

"She was an aide at an embassy or a personal secretary to a general or some such thing, but her real job was to find a good husband, preferably a rich and well-connected Frenchman. That's why her parents had sent her to Saigon and why they were helping her pay for her apartment and her jewels.

"The jewels were what brought my mother and father together. She awoke one night to hear a man's sigh in her bedroom. She opened her eyes and saw a man dropping her diamond earrings into her jewelry box. She gasped and he heard her. He turned around and said, 'Do not be alarmed, mademoiselle.' She demanded to know what he was doing there, and he said, 'I am returning your jewels. I had stolen them, you see, but as I was getting ready to climb out of your window, the moon came out from behind a cloud and her light fell on your face. When I saw your beauty, I could not bring myself to deprive it of its ornaments, so I am returning them.' He held up a little black bag, then emptied it into her jewelry box. 'Adieu, ma jolie,' he said, and he was out of the window and gone in an instant.

"My mother called the police as soon as he was gone, but they were not very concerned. 'Did he take anything?' they asked. 'No,' she said. 'And did he hurt you?' they asked. 'No,' she said again. 'Then why are you bothering us?' they asked. My mother could not believe her ears. 'He broke into my apartment in the middle of the night and scared me half to death!' she yelled. 'He's gone now, isn't he?' said the police. 'Well, then it's just a case of simple trespass. We'll send someone over tomorrow.' Then they hung up on her."

"What horrible police," said Kirstin in shock. She could never picture Officer MacGregor or any of the other officers she knew acting like that!

"That's what my mother said," continued Madame Dragonfly with a smile. "And she said much worse things when she stayed home all the next day waiting for the police to come, but they never did. Something else came, though: a dozen roses with a note in a man's handwriting apologizing for disturbing her and asking her to dinner at one of the best restaurants in Saigon.

"She called the police again and told them that the thief had asked her to dinner. She demanded that they send an officer to arrest the criminal in the restaurant. The police were skeptical about her story and doubted that a burglar would offer to buy his victim dinner at a five star restaurant, but after much yelling and arguing, they finally promised to send an officer.

"The note said to be at the restaurant at 6:00, and she was there at 5:45, waiting outside for the police, but they did not arrive until 6:30. At last, a policeman arrived, looking bored and irritated. She marched in with him in tow and immediately saw my father. 'That's him!' she said. 'Arrest him!' 'Did you break into this young lady's apartment last night?' the policeman asked. 'No,' he said. 'All right then. Sorry to disturb you, Monsieur LeGrand,' said the policeman, and he started to leave. 'But he *did!*' insisted my mother. The officer paid no attention to her. She had been rather spoiled, and she was not used to being ignored. She lost her temper and yelled, 'I demand that you arrest him!' and stamped her foot."

Kirstin winced. "She stamped her foot?" Kirstin hadn't done that since she was a little girl.

Madame Dragonfly laughed. "Yes, she stamped her foot. As I said, she had been spoiled by my grandparents and their servants. Anyway, that got the policeman's attention, and he threatened to arrest her for disturbing the peace. My father got up and pulled a chair out for her. He told her quietly that people were staring and that she was making a scene. Her face got very red and she sat down. As she did, she realized that the policeman had called him by name and must know him. She also realized that he must be paying the police off. That was why they hadn't cared that he had broken into her apartment."

"She must have been so scared," said Kirstin.

"Scared?" said Madame Dragonfly, arching her eyebrows in surprise. "You didn't know my mother. She was a little scared, I suppose, but mostly she was impressed. She was also still mad that he had gotten away with breaking into her apartment. 'You *did* break into my apartment last night,' she said more quietly when they were sitting down. 'No, I didn't,' he said. 'You left your window open. You really shouldn't do that unless your apartment is much higher up than the second story, at least when there are trees and brickwork outside your window that make for an easy climb.'

"Later on, she found out that he had been watching her and had arranged the whole thing. He had never really intended to steal her jewels; they weren't worth the effort from his perspective. He used to joke that if she had slept any more soundly, they never would have met. He had stood there in the dark sighing and dropping her earrings for five minutes before she finally woke up."

"And that made your mom fall in love with him?" asked Kirstin incredulously.

Madame Dragonfly thought for a moment. "I don't know if 'fell in love' is really the right way to describe what happened. He was smart and rich and handsome and she enjoyed being with him. There were other men like that whom she could have married, but my father was always in control wherever he was. He was friends with a general, or had bribed the chief of police, or knew damaging secrets about a powerful businessman. Whatever it took, he was able to do it, and my mother admired that.

"My father was also a spy for the South Vietnamese government. They didn't try to stop him from stealing jewels—as long as he was reasonably discreet about it—so long as he would break into the homes of suspected communists and look for information."

"Why would they want him to spy on communists?" asked Kirstin. "I thought Vietnam was a communist country."

"It is now," explained Madame Dragonfly. "Back then, the northern half of the country was communist and the south half was capitalist. North Vietnam and South Vietnam were at war with each other until 1975, when the North won. Before that, though, the South did everything it could to stop the communists, including silencing anyone in the South who might agree with communist ideas or even just disagreed with the South's government. That was where my father came in. He was willing to do the South's dirty work, even if it meant breaking into the homes of people he knew and turning them in."

That didn't sound like the Pierre LeGrand that Kirstin had met. "Did he change as he got older?"

Madame Dragonfly's mouth twisted slightly, as if she had just taken a bite of something that had surprised her by tasting bad. "Oh, yes, he changed. It wasn't a gradual sort of change like most people go through as they get older. With him it happened all at once. He suddenly went from being my father to being a man my mother and I hardly knew."

"What happened?" asked Kirstin.

Madame Dragonfly glanced over at Kirstin. "He gave up his career as a cat burglar and he suddenly wasn't willing to bribe people or blackmail them anymore."

"What's so bad about that?" asked Kirstin.

"He had a family! He had responsibilities!" said Madame Dragonfly bitterly. "All of a sudden, we had no money and all sorts of people were threatening him and my mother. Someone even tried to kidnap me once. My mother pleaded with my father; I even saw her on her knees once begging him, but he wouldn't listen to her."

"That must have been tough, I mean seeing your parents torn apart like that," said Kirstin. "But, like, weren't you proud of him for doing the right thing?"

She looked at Kirstin with her mouth pressed into a thin line of anger and her eyes full of icy blue daggers. For an instant, Kirstin thought Madame Dragonfly was going to say something incredibly harsh, but she didn't. Her face relaxed slightly after a second and she said, "Was it right for him to tear his family apart? Was it right for him to put his wife and daughter in danger from the people he used to work with, who were extremely vicious, by the way? As you get older, you'll start to understand that right and wrong can be very complicated, particularly in a place like Vietnam and particularly at a time like that when everything was falling apart. The right thing to do would have been to put his family first. Besides, the only people getting hurt were criminals themselves. Everybody was stealing and blackmailing and bribing; my father was just better at it than other people. It's not as if he was stealing from innocent people."

"But it's never right to steal and do that other stuff," persisted Kirstin. "The Bible says that—"

Madame Dragonfly held up her hand. "Do *not* start talking to me about the Bible," she warned. "I've heard plenty about that from my father and Jack Nguyen. I like you, Kirstin, and

I want to keep liking you, so don't start lecturing me on morality and religion." She looked over and saw that she had hurt Kirstin's feelings. "I'm sorry; I shouldn't have snapped at you. I'm just tired of people trying to push Christianity on me. You're a nice girl, Kirstin, and your religion may be fine for you, but it's not for me."

"Did your dad become a Christian?" asked Kirstin. "Is that what happened?"

Madame Dragonfly nodded. "He said he was stealing a jeweled crucifix from a church when the priest caught him. Stealing from a church would have been a serious problem, even for someone with my father's connections, so he was scared. But the priest forgave him and let him go. For some reason, that changed everything for my father. He talked about it for days afterward. He said it was like he had been dying of thirst without knowing it and someone had given him a drink of water. Or he'd say that he'd been living in a cave his whole life and had seen the sun for the first time. He wouldn't shut up about it.

"He started spending lots of time reading the Bible and talking to the priest. It worried my mother, but I kind of liked it at first. He was a lot happier and warmer than he had been before, and he was more fun to be with. That was when he promised me the Autumn Rose. He said he would give it to me when he thought I was ready. He had stolen it about a week before he met the priest, and he knew how I felt about it." She paused. "That was the happiest day of my life. Then the next day he announced to my mother and me that he was giving up 'the business' and things went downhill fast.

"A week later, he disappeared. The day before he left, he

said he was going to give me something even more beautiful and valuable than the Autumn Rose. I asked him what it was, and he handed me a Bible. Then he kissed me goodnight, and I went to bed. That was the last time I saw him.

"The next morning my mother started putting our lives back together. She took care of the problems my father had left behind, married a general in the North Vietnamese army that had just conquered South Vietnam, and moved on."

"Did you ever read it?" asked Kirstin.

"Read what?"

"The Bible he gave you."

Madame Dragonfly shook her head. "Not after I saw what it did to him. Believe it or not, I was scared to death of that book for years. I was afraid it would ruin me the way it ruined my father."

Kirstin was trying to think of a tactful way to say that maybe being "ruined" like her father was not such a bad thing when Madame Dragonfly said, "Ah, there's the White Fish Inn!" It was a big white clapboard building at the end of a little road. A thick pine forest surrounded it on three sides, and the only building nearby was a little gift shop and art gallery connected to the inn by a stone path. Kirstin thought it looked very cozy and peaceful, but she also worried that it would be easy to sneak into at night. No one would see someone creeping through the forest that came right up to the back of the inn, and no one outside the inn would hear if you yelled for help. If someone cut the phone line to the inn, the people inside would be pretty helpless. Kirstin decided not to worry about it, though. If there were a problem, Dat and Vladimir would either take care of it or move them to a different hotel. *It sure is nice to have two top-notch security guards watching out for them,* Kirstin thought. *Without those guys, we could be in real trouble.*

CHAPTER 20

SISTER BAY

R ise and shine!" declared a loud, cheery voice outside Arthur's cell. "It's time for breakfast!" Arthur squinted at his watch with bleary eyes. It was 6:03 in the morning. He had been asleep for only an hour or two before being jolted awake by the police sergeant's voice. "Aren't you hungry, son?" asked the sergeant.

Arthur looked up and saw that the sergeant was holding a large plastic bowl and a spoon. Arthur walked over and took them. The bowl was filled with something that looked like wet cement. "Uh, thanks," he said.

"Let me know if there's any extra oatmeal when you're done," said the sergeant. "We use leftovers to fix cracks in the sidewalk." He smiled as he said it, so Arthur assumed he was joking.

The oatmeal was pretty bad, but Arthur ate it all and even scraped the bowl with his spoon. He hadn't eaten anything since breakfast the day before, and he was ravenous. After he had eaten, Arthur felt better. He was awake, he had something in his stomach, and he would hopefully be getting out of jail soon.

Mr. Nguyen had somehow managed the night before to find Thomas West, the best criminal defense lawyer in Belgium, the town where Arthur was in jail, and persuaded him to represent Arthur. After talking to Arthur and Officer MacGregor, whom he had called at home, Mr. West had called the prosecutor and the judge and gotten them to agree to a bail hearing at 8:30 in the morning. If he could get the judge to agree to let Arthur out on bail, which he thought he could, Arthur would probably be able to be back on the road by 9:30.

But that was three hours away. The guards let Arthur take a much needed shower, brush his teeth, and change his clothes, but after that he had nothing to do but wait and worry. He paced up and down and back and forth across his small cell so much that one of the guards commented that he was going to wear out the paint on the floor. That might not be such a bad thing, Arthur decided. The walls, floor, bars, and ceiling were all covered with a dingy, clumpy gray paint that looked disturbingly like the oatmeal he had eaten for breakfast. A fresh coat of paint was certainly in order, though Arthur suspected that they wanted the paint to look like this and specially ordered it. He tried to distract himself by thinking up names for it: Smog, Gross Gray, and Oatmeal Fantasy were his top three guesses.

Arthur prayed a lot too, and that helped. Though he still felt (and was) stuck and powerless, it helped to remind himself that God was ultimately in control of the whole situation. Still, he desperately wished that he could do something, *anything*, to beat the jeans-and-T-shirt gang.

Other people however were doing something, and that thought also comforted Arthur. Mr. Nguyen was on his way. He had told Arthur he would catch the next Concorde from Paris, which was where he had been staying, to America and then arrange for a private plane to take him to Sturgeon Bay, which had the airport closest to Sister Bay. He would then rent a car and drive to Sister Bay.

All of that would take time, though, and Arthur was not sure when Mr. Nguyen would actually get there. Arthur knew that the Concorde could fly from Paris to New York in two hours and that small planes can fly at one hundred to two hundred miles per hour. Based on that, he tried to figure out how long it would take Mr. Nguyen to reach Sister Bay, but it was no use. There were so many things he didn't know. How long would it be before the next Concorde took off? Would Mr. Nguyen be taking a jet or a propeller plane from New York to Sturgeon Bay? Would he have to stop to refuel? Arthur gave up trying to figure it out.

Officer MacGregor was also doing everything he could. He would almost certainly have called the Wisconsin state police and Sister Bay village police by now. He might be coming up personally to help. He might even have gotten the FBI involved. Meanwhile, all Arthur could do was pace and pray.

Finally, Mr. West called. He had managed to get Arthur out on bail. In addition to the bail money, which Mr. Nguyen had arranged for, Arthur had to pay a fifty dollar impound fee and a $150 towing fee to get his car back. By ten, he was on the road again, heading toward Sister Bay.

Even though Arthur was in a hurry, he made very sure that he didn't break any traffic laws. The last thing he wanted to do was get arrested again. Or at least he didn't break any rules until he got past Sturgeon Bay. Then he heard something on the radio that made him forget his caution.

Arthur was listening to a local station, trying to find out

what the weather would be like in Sister Bay over the next few days. He was half listening to the local news announcements about art fairs, high school football practices, and so forth, when the announcer said, "Police are still hunting for suspects in last night's break-in at the White Fish Inn."

He nearly drove off the road. The announcer then went on to talk about the weather, which Arthur, of course, no longer cared about. Then the announcer started talking about farm prices. "What about the break-in?" Arthur yelled at the radio. But it ignored him and went right on telling him things he didn't want to know.

Arthur was only about fifteen minutes from the White Fish Inn by that time, so he didn't bother pulling over and calling. Instead, he just drove there as fast as he could. He was driving through a lovely countryside of cherry orchards, pine forests, and picturesque lakeshore towns, but he hardly noticed. All he cared about was getting to the White Fish Inn as fast as possible.

When he reached it, he saw a much different sight than Kirstin had seen. Little knots of people were standing around in front of the inn, talking and looking worried and upset. Yellow police tape stretched from one side of the building off into the woods and then back to the building further down. Arthur remembered uncomfortably that the last time he had seen a building with police tape, someone had mysteriously disappeared.

Arthur went inside and asked at the desk about Kirstin and Madame Dragonfly. The man behind the reception desk said, "The records were a mess when I came in this morning, but hold on for a minute and I'll check." He flipped through a stack of index cards and said, "They don't seem to have had reservations for last night. . . . No, wait, here's their card. That's weird. Someone pulled it out of the stack. They're in room 223." He stopped and suddenly became awkward. "Uh, why don't you go on up and talk to the, uh, the police."

The blood drained from Arthur's face. "Where is it?" he asked anxiously.

"It's right up these stairs and to your left," the man answered.

"Thanks," said Arthur over his shoulder as he ran up the steps, taking them two at a time. He reached the top, ran through the doorway to his left, and ran right into a burly policeman. "Whoa! Where do you think you're going?" asked the officer.

"Room 223," answered Arthur breathlessly.

Arthur moved to go past the policeman, but a strong hand grabbed his arm. "No, you're not," said the lawman.

Arthur's spirits sank. Was he being arrested *again?* "How come?" he asked.

"That room is a crime scene," answered the lawman sternly.

"But my sister was staying there!" said Arthur.

"She's not in there now," said the policeman, keeping his grip on Arthur's arm. He saw the frantic look on Arthur's face and said more gently, "We're doing everything we can."

Arthur groaned and closed his eyes. He was too late!

CHAPTER 21

A BRIEF REUNION

Arthur had an idea. He opened his eyes and asked, "Is there a phone I can use?"

The policeman looked at him compassionately, thinking that he was going to call his parents. "Ask at the front desk. If they won't let you use their phone, let me know and I'll take care of it."

"Thanks!" said Arthur. He ran out to his car, grabbed his casebook (which the Belgium police had grudgingly given back to him), and ran back inside. The man behind the front desk said Arthur could use the phone, and he quickly dialed Madame Dragonfly's cell phone number—which he had written down in the casebook on the very day that the Davis Detective Agency had agreed to take the case. It was a little fuzzy from getting wet, but he could still read it.

"Hello?" said a woman's voice after three rings. Arthur let out his breath, which he hadn't realized he had been holding. "Hello?" said the voice, now slightly irritated. He could tell it was Madame Dragonfly. "Who is this, and why are you blowing in my ear?"

"It's Arthur. I thought for sure you'd been captured by those guys. Is Kirstin OK?"

"She's fine," said Madame Dragonfly sharply. "Where are you and what have you been doing?"

"I'm at the White Fish Inn. I drove up this morning as soon as I got out of jail."

"Jail?" exclaimed Madame Dragonfly. "What were you doing in jail? No, tell me later. Let me talk to Dat."

Arthur realized that she had no idea what had happened over the last twenty-four hours. "Dat and Vladimir were kidnapped by the, uh, the bad guys," he blurted out quickly. "I escaped, but I got arrested and they planted drugs in my car. I just got out this morning. And they broke into the White Fish Inn last night, or at least I think it was them."

Madame Dragonfly was silent for a moment as she absorbed what Arthur had just said. "We will stay in public places," she said. "They're less likely to move against us in front of many witnesses. Meet us at Al Johnson's Restaurant immediately."

"OK, where is it?"

"It's right on Route 42," she said. "You can't miss it. It's a big wooden building with a grass roof and goats up there grazing."

"There are goats on the roof?" asked Arthur, but Madame had already hung up.

Arthur thanked the man at the hotel desk for letting him use the phone and asked that he tell the police that he had found his sister and the other person who was supposed to be staying in room 223. Then he got in his car and drove slowly up Route 42, carefully looking at the little wooden shops and restaurants for a sign that said "Al Johnson's." Or for a grass roof with goats.

After about five minutes, Arthur saw Al Johnson's—and laughed. It was a large building made of unpainted logs stacked on top of each other like a log cabin. What made him laugh was the low, gently sloping grass roof that really did have goats on it, calmly eating the grass and ignoring the tourists who stood below pointing at them and taking pictures.

Arthur went inside and found Madame Dragonfly and Kirstin sitting at a table and waiting for him. Their breakfast of Swedish pancakes and lingonberries sat half-finished in front of them, but neither of them was eating. As soon as he sat down, they began bombarding him with questions in low, rapid voices. He told them everything that had happened and answered their questions as best he could. After a while, they slowed down enough for Arthur to ask, "So how did you manage to avoid getting caught at the White Fish Inn?"

"When we got there last night," answered Kirstin, "Madame Dragonfly asked me if I thought it looked like a good place to stay. I said it looked nice, but that it might be a little too lonely and secluded. She agreed, so we stayed at a place closer to town."

"Good thinking," said Arthur. "I'm riding with you guys next time."

"Actually, I don't think you will," said Madame Dragonfly thoughtfully.

"Why is that?" asked Arthur.

"Our plan for today is, of course, to go out to the island, find the Autumn Rose, and come back here," explained Madame Dragonfly in a voice so low Arthur had to lean closer. "We'll need someone to stay here and make sure there's not an ambush waiting for us when we get back. Also, if they see us all go out to the island, they will probably guess that the Autumn Rose is there and come after us. If you stay here, they are less likely to figure it out. They'll probably be content to just watch you until we get back."

Arthur felt the hair on the back of his neck stand up. "Do you think they're watching me now?" he whispered.

"Probably," she said casually. "If I were them, I would have staked out the White Fish Inn when I didn't find us there. When you showed up, they probably followed you here. Unfortunately, I didn't think of that until after you called. We shouldn't have met, but it's too late to worry about that now."

Arthur glanced around nervously. He hated being up against a ruthless enemy that always seemed to be one step ahead of him. "So I get to stay here and be a decoy," he said with a resigned sigh. "Why me?"

Madame Dragonfly looked him in the eyes. "You outran and outsmarted them at the wayside. You're the only one of us who could have done that. You stand the best chance of being able to do it again."

"That really was great how you were able to ditch those guys," added Kirstin.

Arthur sighed again. "Thanks," he said. "OK, I'll stay here." He would have done it anyway, of course, but getting compliments certainly helped take the sting out of being left behind by himself while they dug up the treasure.

CHAPTER 22

ON HIS OWN AGAIN

Half an hour later, Arthur was watching from a distance as Kirstin and Madame Dragonfly steered their rented motorboat toward the little island about half a mile offshore. Then he turned and walked purposefully into town, clutching a guidebook and a notebook in his hand. He stopped every minute or so to flip through the guidebook or scribble something in the notebook. He wasn't really taking notes or going anywhere in particular, but he didn't want to look like he was just waiting for the others to get back.

As Madame Dragonfly had recommended, Arthur stayed in crowded, public places. These weren't hard to find in Sister Bay in the summer. The town was absolutely packed with tourists from Chicago and Milwaukee. As Arthur made his way through what seemed to be one huge crowd, he wondered if anybody was left in either city; they all seemed to have decided to take their vacations at the same time and in the same place.

As Arthur walked around town and made a show of looking for clues, he also kept an eye out for Asian men, particularly wearing jeans and T-shirts. He steered well clear of any he saw, and none of them seemed to notice him or follow him. He was beginning to relax when he noticed an Asian man looking at him. He looked older and smaller than the jeans-and-T-shirt gang members, but he was definitely watching Arthur. Also, he was wearing a jacket even though it was over seventy degrees, which Arthur guessed meant the man was carrying a gun hidden under his coat.

Arthur made a sharp turn and jogged across the street. He glanced back and saw the man trying to dodge between cars to follow him. Arthur ducked into a crowd, then turned into the first building he passed. He found himself in the Sister Bay Public Library, a small building with only one big room of books. Arthur quickly looked around for a place to hide. He spotted some chairs behind a row of bookshelves, grabbed a big book, sat down, and held the book up in front of his face. The book was full of pictures of people doing complicated things with some woman's hair, but Arthur hardly noticed; he was listening as hard as he could for any hint that his pursuer might have followed him into the library.

Arthur heard the door open. Then he heard footsteps coming toward him. He sneaked a peak from behind his book and saw a man walking toward him, but it wasn't the man from the street. It was a pudgy Caucasian man with pale skin and a Chicago Bulls T-shirt that was a little too tight around the stomach. Obviously a tourist, thought Arthur as the man sat down a few chairs behind him and started reading a magazine. Arthur relaxed and went back to pretending to read his book.

Just as he was beginning to think he had escaped, Arthur heard the door open again. He peeked around the side of his book again—and saw the man who had been following him! Arthur ducked his head back behind his book. He didn't think the man had seen him, so hiding was probably still the best plan. Then he heard footsteps coming toward him and the sound of someone sitting down just in front of him. A familiar man's voice said, "Arthur, I didn't know you were interested in hair braiding.'"

Arthur put down his book and for the first time noticed the title: "Beautiful Braids: How to Braid Hair Like a Professional." The Asian man from the street was sitting in front of him with an amused smile on his face. "I, uh," Arthur mumbled sheepishly and nervously. He could feel his face turning red. What was he going to do?

"Jack Nguyen," said the man, holding out his hand. "I recognized you from your picture in the newspaper articles about your last case, but from the look on your face, I don't think you recognize me."

Arthur shook the man's hand and tried to think of a way to test whether he was really Jack Nguyen. "Pleased to meet you," he said automatically. Then he added, "Say, uh, how did you meet Frank MacGregor?"

The man's smile didn't waiver even though he knew perfectly well what Arthur was doing. "Fair enough," he said. "Frank and I were military police in South Vietnam together back during the war. Or at least they called us police. Mostly we just walked around at night carrying guns and telling jokes."

It really was Jack Nguyen! "I'm so glad you're here!" said Arthur with relief.

"Where are the other two?" asked Mr. Nguyen. "Is everything all right?"

Arthur nodded. "I'm here keeping an eye on things and acting as a decoy while Kirstin and Madame Dragonfly are out on the island finding the Autumn Rose."

Mr. Nguyen put his hand on Arthur's arm and glanced around quickly. Then he leaned close to Arthur and whispered, "I know I asked, but try to keep your voice down, and be careful about announcing secrets in public like that."

Arthur looked around the room, then leaned over and whispered back, "Don't worry. All the jeans-and-T-shirt gang are Vietnamese, and I don't see any of them here."

Mr. Nguyen relaxed a little. "Still, try to be a little more careful," he said. "Let's go, I've got some things I'll need your help with."

As soon as they left, Dr. Ivanov put down the magazine he had been pretending to read and got up. He adjusted his Bulls T-shirt, which had bunched up over his stomach for what seemed like the hundredth time, and hurried outside to make a phone call. So they had found the Autumn Rose and were digging it up right now on an island (doubtless the one the two women had been seen heading toward earlier in the day); General Tran would find that very interesting indeed.

CHAPTER 23

THE ISLAND

Kirstin sat in the bow of the boat as Madame Dragonfly steered it out to the island. The noise from the motor and the wind made it impossible to talk, so Kirstin leaned forward and enjoyed the feel of the wind in her hair and the rhythmic bounce of the boat as it ran over the little waves raised by the lake breeze. The bouncing was a little like riding a galloping horse, and Kirstin made a game out of seeing how well she could "ride" the boat. The prow kicked up little plumes of spray every time it hit a wave, wetting Kirstin's arms and hands as she held onto the gunwales, but she didn't mind.

Kirstin watched with growing excitement as the island got closer and closer. It was the same little island she had seen in the picture at Mr. LeGrand's house. The grove of pine trees covering most of the island, the little cabin with the stone chimney, and the pier sticking out into the water were just like they had been in the picture. The only difference was that the big sailboat wasn't there. Kirstin turned and yelled, "No sailboat! Maybe he's not there!" Madame Dragonfly nodded.

Madame Dragonfly slowed the boat down as they came close to the dock and steered the boat up to it. As the prow gently nudged the dock, Kirstin jumped out and tied up the boat.

Then they both unloaded their equipment (two shovels; a metal detector, in case the pearl was buried in a metal box; a tape measure marked in meters; a compass; two sandwiches; three apples; and a big thermos of lemonade) and carried it up the path to the cabin. Madame Dragonfly knocked on the door, but no one answered.

They took out the map and tried to figure out where the red X was. There was no X painted on the ground, of course, so they made a guess after several minutes of looking at the map and the island and trying to figure out where exactly the X was supposed to be. Then they took out the tape measure and the compass and figured out where twenty meters west of the imaginary X was. They took out their shovels and excitedly began to dig.

Twenty minutes later, they were sweaty and tired and not nearly so excited. They stood leaning on their shovels and drinking lemonade as they looked down at a hole in the ground that had contained lots of rocks and tree roots, but no pearl. "Maybe it was a mistake to leave Arthur behind," said Madame Dragonfly when she had gotten her breath back.

Kirstin smiled as she remembered the huge hole Arthur had dug at the horse farm. It had only been two days ago, but it seemed much longer. "His hole digging skills would come in pretty handy right now, wouldn't they?" she said.

"They certainly would," agreed Madame Dragonfly. She leaned her shovel against a tree and added, "Hole digging is harder work than it looks, and before I do any more of it, I'm going to see if I can find anything with the metal detector."

Kirstin watched intently as Madame Dragonfly slowly walked in ever widening circles around the hole, sweeping the head of the metal detector back and forth. A wire ran from the box built into the handle of the detector to thick earphones that Madame Dragonfly wore on her head so she could listen for the tones that would indicate she had found something metallic.

They nearly jumped out of their skins when a loud voice behind them called out, "You won't find anything with that, Diem." Madame Dragonfly looked up sharply and Kirstin gasped as she turned around to see Mr. LeGrand walking toward them from the cabin. "Sorry to startle you. I wasn't sure you could hear me with those headphones on. I know what you're looking for, and you won't find it with that. I put it in a plastic box so that nobody could find it by just searching the island with a metal detector." He noticed the hole they had dug. "I would have told you before you dug that, but I was on the other side of the island and didn't hear you come."

Madame Dragonfly took off her earphones. "So where is it?" she asked.

Mr. LeGrand chuckled and walked over to her. "Why yes, it's good to see you too, Diem. It's been a long time." He reached out to her, but she took a step back from him. Her face was hard as stone. He smiled sadly. "Except for the blue eyes, you look exactly like your mother did the last time I saw her."

Diem LeGrand wanted very much to know what that meant, but she was also Madame Dragonfly, and she kept her eyes and heart hard and repeated, "Where is the Autumn Rose?"

He sighed. "I told you that I would give it to you when you're ready."

She rolled her eyes. "I'm ready. I figured out all your little riddles and clues, with the help of my detectives, of course," she added with a nod toward Kirstin. "I'm here. What more do I need to do?"

He looked at her hard. "And how did you find those clues and riddles?"

She knew she was being tested, but she wasn't sure what the right answer was. "I found the horse farm and went from there."

"I see," he said. "And how did you find the horse farm?"

"On the Internet," she answered. "I searched for 'Autumn Rose,' and its web site came up."

He pursed his lips and nodded, and she could tell by his face that she had failed the test. "Before I left for America, I gave you a Bible. Written in the margin of one of the pages is the address of a post office box in Chicago that I set up so you could reach me without your mother knowing. I checked it every day for twenty years looking for a letter from you.

"I also sometimes used it as an address for the horse farm, so I thought maybe you found the box, traced it to the horse farm, and came in person without writing. It seems I was wrong."

"Mother found the Bible and burned it before I could read it," she said.

He looked her in the eyes, and she dropped her gaze. "You never could lie to me," he said gently.

"But, why do I have to read the Bible in order to get the Autumn Rose, Papa?" asked Diem.

"You have to know God," he answered. "Otherwise, the pearl will be a snare for your heart, as it nearly was for mine. Beautiful and valuable things can take the place of God in our hearts, and the love of them can make us do horrible things. I saw the look in your eyes when you held the Autumn Rose as a schoolgirl. I knew it wasn't safe for you to have it until after God had you."

"So you want me to go back to Vietnam, read the Bible, learn to 'know God'—whatever that means— and then come back for the Autumn Rose?" she asked incredulously.

"I'd prefer that you'd stay here instead of going back to Vietnam, but otherwise, yes," he answered.

She was flabbergasted. "So I came all this way for nothing?"

"Oh, no, not for nothing," he corrected her. "Not for the pearl, perhaps, but for something far more valuable." He gestured toward the cabin. "Why don't we sit down on the porch. The view is excellent, and we have many things to talk about. You're welcome to join us, Kirstin."

Kirstin hesitated and looked at her watch. "That'd be great," she said, "but is this really a safe place to be? I mean, what if those guys who jumped Dat and Vladimir decide to come over here?"

"So the thugs who broke into my house have followed you here," said Mr. LeGrand without great surprise. "I thought they might. I tied up the *Autumn Rose*—the sailboat, not the pearl—on the other side of the island so that it would be possible to leave without being seen from shore. We'll just sail straight across the bay to Michigan, rent a car, and be miles away before they realize we're not here."

"But what about Arthur?" asked Kirstin, worried at the thought of abandoning her brother in a dangerous place.

"Your brother is here too?" asked Mr. LeGrand. Kirstin nodded. He wrinkled his brows in thought. "That does present a problem. Is there any way we can reach him?"

"He probably has his pager on," said Kirstin. "He usually

carries it when we're working." She snapped her fingers. "In fact, I know he's got it. I gave him some fresh batteries this morning because his old ones got ruined when he got his pager wet while he was running away from those guys."

Madame Dragonfly paged Arthur from her cell phone, and he called back a few minutes later. She told him briefly what had happened and about her father's idea of sailing to the other side of the bay. Arthur then told her that he had run into Mr. Nguyen and that they were now working together to figure out the best way to evade their pursuers and find Dat and Vladimir. She then talked to Mr. Nguyen for several minutes, and they decided that the best plan was for her, her father, and Kirstin to sail to Michigan while Arthur and Mr. Nguyen pretended to be waiting for them back in Sister Bay. Meanwhile, Arthur and Mr. Nguyen would do what they could to find Dat and Vladimir. The two teams would then work together to rescue the bodyguards and hopefully put their kidnappers in jail. Their plans would have been much different if they had known that Dr. Ivanov had overheard Arthur's conversation with Mr. Nguyen in the library. But, of course, they didn't know about that.

CHAPTER 24

THE AUTUMN ROSE

Mr. LeGrand packed a small suitcase, shut up his cabin, and took his two guests across the island to a second dock, where the *Autumn Rose* was tied up. Kirstin decided it was the loveliest boat she had ever seen. It had a long, gracefully curved blue hull that looked just perfect for racing through the water before a strong summer wind. One tall mast rose out of a spotless white wooden deck, its sail furled. A little red cabin stood just in front of the mast, and inside Kirstin glimpsed an old-fashioned wooden ship's wheel. Once when the Davises were vacationing by the sea, Kirstin had heard an old sailor reminisce lovingly about a beautiful ship he had sailed on once. He had said it was "a lady, a real lady." That had confused Kirstin, but now she knew what he meant. The *Autumn Rose* was a real lady.

Mr. LeGrand asked Kirstin and Madame Dragonfly to wait onboard while he got one last thing. He disappeared for about ten minutes, then came back breathing hard and carrying a very dirty plastic toolbox. He set it down on the deck while he unfurled the sail and cast off the ropes holding them to the dock.

Kirstin and Madame Dragonfly had been chatting about the boat, but they fell silent when they caught sight of the box Mr. LeGrand was carrying. It sat there on the deck begging to be opened and making it impossible for them to think about anything else. Kirstin and Madame Dragonfly exchanged looks. Madame Dragonfly asked, "Is that it?"

"That's it," said Mr. LeGrand. He picked up the box and took it down into the cabin.

"May I look at it?" his daughter called after him.

He stopped on the stairs just inside the cabin door. Then he turned and studied her face for a moment. There was a longing in her eyes that was almost a sadness. "All right," he said, "but just for a minute."

He brought the box back out onto the deck and opened it. Inside was a bundle of yellowed, musty smelling cloth. He took it out and carefully unrolled it. Lying nestled in the center was something round and black. It was larger than a golf ball, but smaller than a tennis ball, and it had a sort of sheen or iridescence whenever the sunlight touched it.

She picked it up carefully and slowly held it up to the sun. Her face was filled with radiant joy, and all the Madame Dragonfly polish and hardness melted away. It was the first time Kirstin had seen her look truly happy. But Kirstin noticed that the longing and sadness did not completely leave her face. Her father noticed it too. "It's like looking at a picture of a beautiful place you can never visit, isn't it?" he said with a gentle smile on his face. "A beautiful place you've never been to, but that you miss desperately."

"Yes," said Diem with a startled expression, "yes, that's it exactly. How did you know?"

"Because that's how I felt when I first looked at it," he said, "and because you and I are very much alike in some ways, or at least we used to be."

"What do you mean?" asked Diem with just a trace of suspicion in her voice.

He thought for a moment. Then he said, "Now I know how to get to the beautiful place in the picture. In some ways, I'm already there."

"What do you mean?" asked Diem again.

"The place in the picture is the kingdom of God," he said. "I know that one day there will be a physical kingdom and that I will be in it, but even now the kingdom of God is within me." He saw the confusion in Diem's face. "It's hard for me to explain," he said apologetically. "Imagine that you are looking at a stained glass window in the dark. It's hard to make out and not very attractive. Then imagine that the sun comes up and you see for the first time all the beautiful glowing colors and you understand what the window was meant to be. That's what it's like to have the kingdom of God inside you. Your life becomes filled with beauty and meaning as the light of God fills you." He looked over at his daughter. "That's what you were meant for, Diem. That's what we were all meant for.

"You can't enter the kingdom without becoming a subject of the King, of course, and that's not easy." He looked out over the waves for a moment. Diem sat watching him silently, waiting for him to continue. "For me it meant losing my home, my family, and almost my life, but that was a small price to pay. Jesus Himself probably put it best when he said that 'the kingdom of heaven is like a merchant seeking beautiful pearls, who, when he had found one pearl of great price, went and sold all that he had and bought it.' That's actually the verse I wrote the Chicago address next to."

"I see," said Diem slowly. "I had never really thought of it that way. I always thought Christianity was mostly about rules, not about . . ." She held up the Autumn Rose and looked at it again, losing herself in its beauty. "Not about something like this."

"Christianity is mostly about love," said her father. "God's love for us and our love for Him and for those around us. The rules really only come in because of His love for us, the same way your mother and I set rules for you when you were little because we loved you."

A cloud came over Diem's face. "If you loved me, Papa, why did you leave?" she asked in French. "And why didn't you ever come back or even write?"

Kirstin knew enough French to understand some of what Diem said and was curious to hear how Mr. LeGrand would answer, but she also knew that Diem intended the conversation to be private. "I, uh, I'll be up front if you need me," Kirstin said. She got up and walked to the bow, where she leaned against the rail and looked out at the bay as she thought about what she had just heard.

Meanwhile, Mr. LeGrand was saying to his daughter, "I would have stayed if I could have. And once I left, I couldn't come back. I did write to you, but I knew your mother would never give you the letters."

"Why did you have to leave?" she asked.

He hesitated. "This probably won't be easy for you to hear," he warned.

"Do you think not knowing all these years has been easy?" she countered. "I want to know the truth."

"All right." He took a deep breath. "The truth is that your mother betrayed me. The North Vietnamese were coming for me that night. If I had stayed, they would have killed me."

Diem gasped. "Why would she do something like that?"

"We were playing both sides of the field," he explained. "I was secretly working for the South against the North, and she was secretly working for the North against the South. Whichever side won, we would be on the winning team. But when I became a Christian, I decided that breaking into people's homes and going through their papers was wrong, so I stopped working for the South. As you can guess, that made me some powerful enemies. I also stopped stealing, and that made me more enemies.

"So suddenly I had lots of enemies and no friends. Your mother felt I was letting her down and needlessly putting her and you in danger. I wasn't an asset to her anymore, I was a liability. From her perspective, I wasn't willing to help her anymore."

"But turning you over to the North would help her," said Diem. "She would be giving them one of the South's spies, and she would also be proving how dedicated she was to their cause." He nodded. Diem didn't want to believe it, but it made sense in a brutal way. She also knew deep down that it sounded like something her mother might do. She saw that his eyes were full of sadness and remembered pain, and she knew he was telling the truth. Then she remembered the post office box in Chicago. "You saw it coming, didn't you? You knew she was going to betray you. That's why you set up the post office box and put the address in the Bible you gave me."

He nodded. "She surprised me by how fast she did it, but yes, I knew."

"So why didn't you beat her to the punch? Why didn't you turn her in to the South before she turned you in to the North?"

Diem asked. She had a general idea of what his answer would be, but she wanted to hear him say it.

"I thought about it," he said. "In fact, I almost did it when I first figured out what she was doing." He shook his head at the memory. "I was furious."

"So what stopped you?" she persisted.

He shrugged. "I didn't know a lot about Christianity back then, but I knew Christ said that we have to love and forgive our enemies. In fact, He said that if we don't forgive those who sin against us, God won't forgive us our sins. I was just starting to realize how much there was for God to forgive in me, and I really wanted to be forgiven. Turning her in wouldn't exactly have been loving and forgiving, so I didn't see how I could do it."

They were both silent for a moment, and Diem realized where the conversation was likely to lead next. She didn't want to talk about that, at least not yet. "I'll go get Kirstin," she said, and she got up and walked away.

A moment later, she reappeared with Kirstin behind her. "Can I look at it now?" Kirstin asked.

"Certainly," said Mr. LeGrand. He took it back out of the plastic box and handed it to her. The pearl was warm and smooth in her palm. It was black, but its surface held hints of other colors, as if a rainbow was hiding in it. As she held it and turned it, she noticed that there was something about it that tricked her eyes. It seemed like she was looking *into* it, not just *at* it. It seemed like a little round window into an endless night, but with the promise of a brilliant morning of flashing colors beyond.

Then Kirstin held the Autumn Rose up to the sun, and the

morning came. It completely took her breath away. Gold, ruby, orange like a warm fire, and other colors she had never imagined and couldn't even begin to name shone out in a glorious ring around the pearl. "It's beautiful!" she gasped. "It's like . . . like . . . ," she struggled for words to describe it, "like a halo or . . . or like a sunrise in heaven."

"That's how it got its name," said Mr. LeGrand. "The pearl was found hundreds of years ago by a pearl diver who lived in a little Christian village by the South China Sea. He gave it to the priest of the village church. When the priest saw it, he said, 'The rose that blooms in autumn is most rare and beautiful, for it defies the winter and gives promise of the spring that lies beyond.' He meant that the deep black of the pearl symbolized death and the beautiful light symbolized life after death. He named it the Autumn Rose, and everyone in the village came to look at it. A local nobleman heard about it and ordered his soldiers to take it and bring it to his palace."

"How terrible!" said Kirstin. "I can't believe that guy just stole it from the priest!"

Mr. LeGrand shrugged. "Later on, the Chinese emperor stole it from the nobleman—or he told the nobleman that he admired it and wished he had one like it, which was basically the same thing because not giving it to the emperor would have cost the nobleman his head. When the emperor died, the pearl was buried with him, but it was stolen by a grave robber. A warlord stole it from him, and, well you get the picture. It's been stolen by a lot of people."

"Including you," said Kirstin without thinking. Her hand flew to her mouth. "Oh! I am so sorry! That was totally rude of me!"

"Including me," agreed Mr. LeGrand with a smile. "Don't be sorry. It's true; I did steal it. A Major Tran in the North Vietnamese army had seen it before the war in the home of a Saigon gangster. He had heard about me through my wife, and he offered me a million dollars to steal it and sneak it to him in the North. I stole it for him, but once I saw it, I couldn't bear to give it up. I told him the deal was off, and I returned the money, but he wouldn't take no for an answer. He threatened to kill me when I still wouldn't give it to him."

"Wow!" said Kirstin. "It sure has an effect on people." She handed the pearl back to him gingerly.

"Money and beauty will do things to people," he said as he wrapped it up and put it back in its box. "Once I became a Christian, I thought I should give it back, but to whom? I knew the gangster had stolen it, but I didn't know who he stole it from. And the village that it came from was long gone. Then I saw how Diem looked at it, and I decided to give it to her when she was ready. It might be a little dangerous for her to have, but she was tough and smart and could take care of herself, so I wasn't too worried."

"What was Major Tran's first name?" asked Diem suddenly.

"I think it was Cao," said Mr. LeGrand. He thought for a moment. "Yes, it was. Major Cao Tran." He caught the look in her eyes. "You think he's behind this, don't you?"

She nodded. "He's a general now. I think he commands a military intelligence unit."

He took a deep breath and let it out. "I suspected as much. Those thugs who broke into my house acted like military intelligence types; brutal, thorough, and efficient, but not very creative."

"How did you escape from them?" asked Kirstin.

He smiled slyly. "Let's just say that I'm very hard to surprise and even harder to catch. Just because I stopped being a burglar doesn't mean I forgot everything I knew."

"So what do you think they'll do next?" asked Kirstin. But as soon as the words were out of her mouth, she was able to answer her own question. She had been looking back toward the island as they talked, using a little set of sightseeing binoculars she had brought with her. Suddenly she saw a man standing on the crest of the island holding his own set of binoculars and looking straight at her! A second later, he was pointing at the *Autumn Rose* and she could see that he was shouting to someone behind him. Then he jumped down and disappeared. "They're on the island! They've spotted us!" Kirstin said breathlessly.

"How many of them are there?" asked Diem.

"What are they doing?" asked Mr. LeGrand.

Kirstin scanned back and forth across the island with her binoculars. "I can't see them now." Something caught her eye at the edge of the island. "Hold on a second," she said. A speedboat came into view, then another. Both boats were full of men with guns, and they were headed straight for the *Autumn Rose!* Kirstin gulped. "Here they come!"

CHAPTER 25

THE NEED FOR SPEED

Arthur and Mr. Nguyen sat on a bench on the dock back in Sister Bay, enjoying the early afternoon sun. They had just had an excellent lunch at the Northern Door Café, and they were now making a show of waiting for Kirstin and Madame Dragonfly to return. Mr. Nguyen had a pair of powerful binoculars that he was pretending to use to watch the island. In reality, he was watching a fisherman about halfway between them and the island, and he was giving a running commentary on the man's success. "The jig isn't working, so he's switching to worms." He shook his head. "Worms," he said derisively. "Where is the sport in that? He might as well use depth charges."

"No sign of the jeans-and-T-shirt gang, huh?" said Arthur, who was not a fisherman and thought that the only thing more boring than fishing was listening to people talk about fishing.

"Oh, there's two of them watching us from a car parked beside the road," said Mr. Nguyen nonchalantly. "They're being pretty obvious about it. Didn't you see them?" His voice grew more excited, and he leaned forward. "Ah, he has one on, and it's a big one! Look at the rod bend!"

"What?" said Arthur nervously, turning to look for the car. "Where are they?"

"Stop that!" ordered Mr. Nguyen. "If they know we see them, they'll hide better and we may not be able to spot them."

"I guess you're right," said Arthur uncomfortably. "It's just kind of creepy knowing someone is watching you."

"It is," agreed Mr. Nguyen. "You've got to learn to take your mind off it. Maybe you could try taking an interest in fishing. . . . He's got the net out. The fish is almost to the boat. He's almost got him now." He winced. "Oh! The line broke."

As Arthur half-listened to Mr. Nguyen, he idly watched the boats on the lake. He saw two speedboats shoot away from a dock about two hundred yards down the lakeshore. "Wonder what they're in such a hurry about," he muttered to himself.

"What was that?" asked Mr. Nguyen.

Arthur didn't answer right away. He had just noticed that both speedboats were full of men with black hair and olive skin. He also noticed that they were headed straight for the island! "Those boats! I think that's the jeans-and-T-shirt gang!"

"Where?" asked Mr. Nguyen, giving Arthur the binoculars.

Arthur pointed and held the binoculars to his eyes. "It's them all right! And they're taking guns out of big duffel bags. I see AK-47s, M-16s, handguns—"

"Get down!" yelled Mr. Nguyen. He knocked Arthur to the dock a split second before a bullet blew a piece out of the back of the bench they had been sitting on. In one fluid motion, Mr. Nguyen rolled into a kneeling position behind the bench, pulled out his pistol, and aimed it at a car sitting beside a deserted stretch of road behind them. Bang! Bang! Bang! Mr. Nguyen fired three quick shots. One of the car's windows shattered and a bullet hole appeared in one of its doors. Its tires squealed, and it sped away.

"They weren't just there to watch us," Mr. Nguyen said as he and Arthur got up. "They were there to make sure we didn't interfere if we noticed the speedboats." He shook his head in self-disgust. "I can't believe I didn't realize that!

"Let's get out of here," he said, scanning the lakefront. "Those guys aren't finished with us. Grab that suitcase." He gestured toward a bulky, black metal box with a plastic handle. Arthur picked it up and was surprised at how heavy it was.

They hurried along the dock, Arthur lugging the suitcase and Mr. Nguyen holding the gun in front of him and looking for attackers. Suddenly Arthur had an idea. He stopped in front of a group of frightened-looking young men standing by their boat. It was a lean, black craft with a big inboard motor. *The Need for Speed* was painted in white forward-leaning letters on the boat's side. "Mr. Nguyen!" Arthur called. "What do you think?"

Mr. Nguyen turned and looked back. A smile spread across his face. "Excellent idea, Arthur," he said as he jogged over. The young men backed away as he came over. "Gentlemen," said Mr. Nguyen in a polite, friendly voice, "may we borrow your boat?"

"Uh, yeah sure," said one of the men nervously, his eyes darting between Mr. Nguyen's friendly face and the gun dangling casually from his hand. "Whatever you want."

"Thank you very much!" said Mr. Nguyen. "Arthur, put the suitcase in the boat." He turned back to the men. "We'll return it shortly. May I have the keys?"

"Here you go," said the man who had spoken as he gingerly handed Mr. Nguyen the keys. "Keep it as long as you want."

"You are too kind," said Mr. Nguyen pleasantly as he got

into the boat. Then he turned to Arthur. "Do you know how to drive a boat like this?"

"I, uh, I think so," said Arthur. His father had taught him how to drive a boat with an inboard motor when the family had gone water-skiing earlier in the summer. The dashboard of *The Need for Speed* looked basically the same as the one on the boat Arthur had driven then, but there were a lot more dials and buttons on this one.

"Good," said Mr. Nguyen. "Catch!" he added as he tossed Arthur the keys. "You drive. I'll sit back here and—" He was interrupted by a bullet smashing into the stern of the boat. He saw at once where the shot had come from; the car he had shot at earlier had pulled up on shore about thirty yards away, and he could see a rifle barrel sticking out of its passenger side window. He aimed his pistol, but did not fire because there were people near the car who might get hurt if he missed. Instead, he held up the metal suitcase as at least a partial shield for him and Arthur, and he yelled, "Go! Go!"

Arthur frantically pulled loose the last rope and gunned the engine. The boat sped away from the dock as another two shots rang out. One bullet buried itself in the dock beside the boat, and the other crashed through the side of the boat and missed Mr. Nguyen by inches.

In a few seconds, they were out of range and racing toward the island. Their enemies had gotten there first, but they had already discovered that their prey was gone. Arthur could see tiny figures with guns jumping into the two speedboats and pulling away from the dock. He turned to tell Mr. Nguyen, but the words died in his throat.

Smoke was pouring from the housing for the motor! One

of the bullets that hit the boat must have caused a gasoline leak, and now the gas had caught fire! Mr. Nguyen was spraying the engine with a small fire extinguisher, but it didn't seem to be having much effect. The extinguisher ran out as Arthur watched. Mr. Nguyen shook it, tried it again unsuccessfully, and dropped it on the floor. He sat down and began calmly but quickly taking complicated-looking pieces of metal and plastic out of the suitcase and connecting them together. He saw Arthur staring back at him and said, "Watch where you're going!"

Arthur turned around just in time to see a big rock sticking out of the water right ahead of them! He yanked the wheel to the right and just barely missed smashing them to bits on the rock. He noticed that he couldn't see the two speedboats anymore. He looked wildly around, then realized that they must be behind the island. They must have spotted the *Autumn Rose*. He groaned and his heart sank. What chance would a sailboat have of outracing two speedboats?

"We'll just have to get there first," Arthur said to himself as they roared past Mr. LeGrand's isle with its cozy cabin and shady grove of pines. Once they were around the island, Arthur could see the speedboats about a hundred yards ahead of them. About three hundred yards beyond the lead speedboat, a blue-hulled sailboat was running before the wind with all its sails out and stretched tight. He could just make out the words "Autumn Rose" on her stern.

The Need for Speed was a fast boat, and they were gaining on the other two boats, but Arthur wasn't sure they would reach them before they reached the *Autumn Rose*. He suddenly realized that they didn't have a plan for what to do when they got there, or at least that he didn't know what the plan was. How were they going to deal with two boats full of men with machine guns? He turned and yelled over the roar of the motor, "What do we do when we get there?"

But before Mr. Nguyen could answer, the motor died. Arthur tried to restart it, but it was no good. The heat from the fire had melted some of the wiring, and there was nothing he could do. Everything was suddenly silent in *The Need for Speed*, except for the crackle of the fire in the engine housing and the buzz from the motors of the two other speedboats as they rapidly grew further away from them and closer to the *Autumn Rose*.

CHAPTER 26

THE CHASE

As soon as Kirstin spotted the speedboats, the *Autumn Rose* burst into a flurry of activity. Mr. LeGrand turned the boat so that the wind was directly behind them and they could run before it at top speed. As soon as he had set the wheel, he ran back up on deck to let out as much sail as possible, darting around the boat with the speed and agility of a cat. Kirstin knew next to nothing about sailboats, but she helped as much as possible, holding ropes, keeping an eye on their course and the wind, and so forth. The wind picked up some too, and soon they were racing over the waves, white foam curling away from the sailboat's sharp prow.

They were going as fast as they could, but it wasn't fast enough. Kirstin turned and looked behind them. Despite her and Mr. LeGrand's hard work, the speedboats were closer—a lot closer. She looked ahead and saw that the northern shore of the bay was still just a line on the horizon. There was just no way that they would be able to reach it before the speedboats caught them.

Meanwhile, Diem had been on the radio talking to the police and Coast Guard. Kirstin could hear her using her best Madame Dragonfly manner, but she seemed to be getting nowhere. "Well if you don't have speedboats, who does? . . . That's not good enough! By the time they get here from Sturgeon Bay, it will be too late! Surely you have a helicopter? . . . Well get it out of the shop! . . . Look, anything that will take more than five minutes to get here will take too long! . . . Well, if you can't, this will be all over the front page of tomorrow's paper with your name on it! Don't you think the newspapers monitor this radio channel?" She switched off the radio without waiting for an answer and turned to her father and Kirstin, her face a mask of frustration. "The earliest the police or the Coast Guard can get here is half an hour from now."

"Well, I guess it's up to us to figure something out," said Kirstin. "Do we have any guns or anything?"

He shook his head. "All I've got is a flare gun."

That gave Kirstin an idea. "Do you have any gasoline?"

He and Diem both saw at once what she was getting at. "There's a plastic jug of it down by the auxiliary motor," he said.

"I'll go get it," called Diem from the cabin. "Good thinking, Kirstin!" A moment later, she appeared with a red plastic five gallon jug. She and Kirstin emptied it into the water behind the boat as Mr. LeGrand went to find the flare gun. The first speedboat was close enough now so that the men in it could see what they were doing. A couple of them pointed and said something, but the boat didn't steer out of the way.

Mr. LeGrand returned with the flare gun just as the lead boat was coming into the gasoline slick. He fired, and the burning flare shot straight into the slick! The gasoline caught fire, but the flames only burned for a few seconds, and they weren't very high. The speedboats drove right through the fire unharmed. Kirstin could see the men in them laughing.

"What do we do now?" asked Diem as the boats got closer and closer.

No one said anything for a few seconds. They were all out of ideas. Then Mr. LeGrand said, "We pray."

A few seconds later, the lead speedboat was only twenty yards away. Then to their amazement, a jagged hole about a foot across and two feet long suddenly appeared in the bottom of its hull as it bounced up off a wave. When it came down, the rushing water tore at the hole and the boat disintegrated! Men, guns, and pieces of boat splashed into the water.

"How—" began Kirstin in astonishment. Before she could finish her sentence, though, the back of the second speedboat exploded in a red and orange fireball! The men in it were thrown into the water. A pillar of black smoke rose into the sky as the boat burned and sank.

The three of them stood frozen on the deck of the *Autumn Rose,* silent and slack-jawed in shock. They could hardly believe their eyes. What had happened? Diem recovered first. "Wow, Papa!" she said. "You're going to have to teach me to pray like that!"

He smiled at his daughter's joke, then he chuckled, then he laughed hard. Kirstin started to laugh too, and then Diem joined in. Soon they were all laughing so hard their sides hurt and they could hardly stand up. It felt so wonderful to laugh after their incredible escape that they didn't want to stop.

They all stopped after just a few seconds, though, when they heard another explosion. They looked back and saw the remains of a black speedboat far behind them engulfed in flames and rapidly sinking. All three of them became somber in an instant, and Kirstin felt suddenly terrified, as if the burning boat should mean something very frightening to her. "What happened?" she asked, but none of them knew the answer.

CHAPTER 27

A REALLY BIG GUN

This is what had happened. As soon as Arthur realized that the motor was dead, he got ready to jump overboard. With no wind to blow the fire back and away from the boat, flames were now darting out of the sides of the engine housing and advancing toward the gas tank. Arthur wanted to be as far away from *The Need for Speed* as possible when the fire reached the gasoline. Just as he was ready to dive over the side, though, Mr. Nguyen yelled, "No! Wait!"

Arthur turned and saw for the first time what Mr. Nguyen had been assembling in the back of the boat. The small Vietnamese man was straining to maneuver a huge and complicated-looking rifle so that its barrel rested on the boat's gunwale. Arthur had never seen anything like the gun before. It was at least five feet long, and it must have weighed over forty pounds. At its base, the barrel was almost as thick as Arthur's wrist. "That's a really big gun," observed Arthur.

"Yes, it is," panted Mr. Nguyen, "and I'll need your help if I'm going to be able to use it."

Arthur didn't know much about rifles, but he could see that this one had a bolt action, and he remembered from his experience at summer camp several years ago that bolt action rifles could not be fired very rapidly. "But you'll only have time for a few shots," said Arthur, "and there's at least a dozen of them."

"This is for shooting boats, not men," replied Mr. Nguyen. "Now get down here. We only have a few seconds!" Arthur glanced nervously at the flames. They were only a foot from the gas tank, and Arthur felt uncontrollable fear welling up inside him. When he was a child, he had once seen a man on fire after a car crash, and he had woken up with terrible nightmares about being burned alive for weeks after that. But he gulped back his fear and went to help Mr. Nguyen. "Hand me one of those bullets, Arthur," he said, pointing to the open suitcase. Arthur pulled out a shell as long as his hand and gave it to Mr. Nguyen, who was looking through the telescope and adjusting the sights on the gun. He glanced at it and handed it back. "No, no, one of the ones with hollow points."

Arthur searched the bag, then found one with a flat point with a hole in the middle and handed it to Mr. Nguyen, who quickly slid it into the firing chamber and slid the bolt up and over to ready the gun for firing. He braced his foot against the opposite side of the boat and leaned forward so the recoil from the gun wouldn't knock him over. Arthur had heard Officer MacGregor talk about hollow-point bullets, and he knew that they mushroomed out when they hit their target to make the biggest hole possible. *How big a hole would that one make?* he wondered.

Mr. Nguyen took a deep breath, then let it out slowly. He pulled the trigger as he was breathing out, and a huge BANG! echoed across the lake and shook the boat. Arthur looked expectantly at the speedboats, but nothing happened. It had missed! Arthur glanced over and saw that the fire was only a few inches from the gas tank.

Mr. Nguyen adjusted the gunsight again and pulled back the bolt, opening the firing chamber and causing the still smoking empty casing to pop out. "Hand me another hollow-point," he said calmly. Arthur wiped the sweat from his palms and handed another bullet to Mr. Nguyen. He loaded the gun and aimed again. Arthur took out another bullet and turned his eyes to the speedboats, making a conscious effort not to look at the fire. He didn't want to know how close it was to the gas.

BANG! For a second, Arthur thought Mr. Nguyen had missed again. Then the lead speedboat flew into pieces as it hit the water, like a snowball hitting a wall. "Yes!" shouted Arthur as he handed Mr. Nguyen the next bullet. He made the mistake of looking at the gas tank, and he saw the flames licking up its side. He took out another bullet and held it tight in his hand as he bit his lip and fought the urge to jump over the side and swim away as fast as he could.

BANG! The bullet must have hit the gas tank on the second speedboat, because it suddenly exploded in a ball of fire. A split second later a loud boom reached Arthur's ears. It was over, and they had won! They had beaten the jeans-and-T-shirt gang and saved Kirstin, Madame Dragonfly, and Mr. LeGrand!

Arthur was so eager to get out of the boat that he didn't even let out a victory yell. He dropped the bullet he was holding and jumped up onto the edge of the boat. Then something made him look back, and he saw Mr. Nguyen desperately pulling on his right leg. His foot had gotten jammed between the side of the boat and the base of one of the seats. The recoil from the gun must have wedged it in like that, Arthur realized. "Jump, Arthur, jump!" shouted Mr. Nguyen with a hopeless look in his eyes.

The flames were all around the gas tank now, but Arthur forced himself to get back into the boat. He braced himself against the deck, grabbed Mr. Nguyen around the chest, and pulled as hard as he could, while Mr. Nguyen pushed with his left foot. Arthur thought he saw the seat base give a tiny bit. He pulled again, straining every muscle in his body. Mr. Nguyen cried out in pain, but his foot popped free!

Mr. Nguyen tried to stand, but nearly fell when he put weight on his right foot. Arthur caught him as he fell and pushed him over the side. Then Arthur dove over himself and swam down into the cold lake water to protect himself from the blast that would come any second on the surface.

He had only been in the water for a few seconds when he heard and felt the explosion. The shock wave hit him like a giant hand at the same time he heard an overpowering WHUMP! and a bright yellow-orange light filled the water around him. He saw black spots and nearly lost consciousness from the violence of the blast.

Arthur shook his head to clear the spots from his eyes and swam weakly to the surface. He felt the heat from the fire and turned to see *The Need for Speed* burning like a torch. "That guy's going to be really mad about his boat," he said to himself.

"You think so?" said a voice behind him. "I had hoped he might not notice."

Arthur turned around and saw Mr. Nguyen treading water with a big smile on his face. "Not much chance of that," Arthur said, wearing a wide grin of his own. "Nice shooting."

"Thanks," said Mr. Nguyen. Then his face grew a little more serious. "And thank you for saving my life." He winced, "Though I think you broke my foot."

"I'm sorry," Arthur said reflexively.

Mr. Nguyen laughed. "Don't be sorry. Having my foot broken certainly beats the alternative."

Arthur noticed for the first time that they were at least a mile from shore. How could Mr. Nguyen swim all that way with a broken foot? "How are we going to get back to shore?" he asked.

"Fortunately, I have my waterproof cell phone with me. Very useful during the monsoon season." He reached into his watery coat pocket and pulled out a plastic bag with a cell phone in it. He paddled over to a seat cushion that had been blown into the water and used it to support himself while he dialed and talked. "Hello, Madame," he said. He listened for a moment, then smiled and said, "So you liked my Armalite .50 caliber? Handy gun, isn't it? I brought it because it was the most powerful thing I could legally bring into the U.S." He listened again for a few seconds. "Actually, we're in the water about four hundred yards behind you. Our boat blew up. Would you mind picking us up?" He paused again. "Thanks." He turned off the phone and put it back in its bag.

They both watched in silence as the *Autumn Rose* turned and sailed over to pick them up, gliding gracefully through the gently rolling waves. The water was cold, but the sun was warm and bright. The remains of *The Need for Speed* rolled over and sank, extinguishing the fire. The only sounds that broke the silence were the lake breeze and the intermittent buzz of far-off unhappy Vietnamese voices yelling at each other. It was the sweetest music Arthur had ever heard.

CHAPTER 28

WHAT BECAME OF THE JEANS-AND-T-SHIRT GANG

Two police boats arrived from Sturgeon Bay about fifteen minutes after Arthur and Mr. Nguyen clambered on board the *Autumn Rose*. The five of them watched from the sailboat with immense satisfaction as the police fished General Tran and ten other men out of the lake. Some of them resisted and some didn't, and two of them had actually swum halfway to shore before they were caught, but eventually they were all sitting on the deck of one of the boats with their hands cuffed behind them. General Tran appeared to be speaking energetically and angrily to the police while the others sat in sullen silence. No one on the *Autumn Rose* could hear what the general was saying, of course, but it couldn't be very important, because the police on the boat were obviously ignoring him.

Whatever General Tran had been saying on the boat, it probably did not include an explanation for what the police found in the hotel rooms in which he and his men had been staying. They found explosives, assault rifles, forged passports, drugs, and a number of other highly illegal items. They also found a surprised Dr. Ivanov, who had been watching old Clint

179

Eastwood movies in his hotel room while he waited for the others to return.

General Tran and his men were trained soldiers and grimly kept their mouths shut in jail despite the threat of spending a very long time there. Dr. Ivanov, however, did not handle pressure well. As soon as he realized that he might wind up spending the rest of his life in jail, he became very cooperative and started telling the police everything they wanted to know. In fact, he talked so much that eventually the police had to tell him to stop because they had all the information they needed for the present.

By the end of the day, the police had raided a small rented cabin, which Dr. Ivanov had told them about, and arrested two more of General Tran's men. They also found Dat and Vladimir, who were heavily drugged, but otherwise fine. Milwaukee police caught the last two members of the jeans-and-T-shirt gang the next day at the airport as they attempted to leave the country using fake passports.

Based on Dr. Ivanov's confession and the evidence the police found in the hotel rooms, it appeared that General Tran had been spying on Diem for some time for unrelated reasons. They had managed to bug her cell phone and heard Diem's first conversation with Arthur and Kirstin and several of the ones that followed. Once he knew they were on the trail of the Autumn Rose, he quickly pulled together a team of his best and most ruthless men and had sent them to America. He promised them that they would be well paid if they could find the Autumn Rose first. When they did not succeed quickly, he came himself with more men, including Dr. Ivanov.

General Tran had meant to keep this all secret, of course,

but now it became very, very public. When news leaked out that a Vietnamese general, fourteen of his men, and a Russian doctor had been caught conducting a secret mission in Wisconsin and breaking all sorts of laws, the press came in droves. Soon newspaper reporters, TV reporters, and magazine reporters from all over the country were in Sister Bay. General Tran's name and picture (in which he looked extremely unhappy) and the story of what he had done were soon prominently displayed on newspapers, TV sets, and magazines nationwide.

The Vietnamese government was furious. This incident embarrassed them badly and came just as they were trying to negotiate a trade treaty with the United States. Vietnam's government spokesman quickly held a press conference and claimed, correctly, that his government knew nothing about what General Tran and his men had been doing, and demanded that they be returned to Vietnam for "a full and fair trial."

General Tran and his men knew that whatever the Vietnamese government said, they would be shot quickly and quietly as soon as they were back in Vietnam. They therefore pleaded with the American law enforcement authorities to be kept in jail. The county judge handling their case was a little surprised to hear criminals actually asking to stay in jail, but he saw no reason to deny their request. General Tran was sentenced to eighty years in prison without the possibility of parole, and his men were given fifty years each.

Dr. Ivanov was also given a fifty year prison sentence, but, because of his cooperation with the police, it was suspended on the condition that he leave the United States and never return. If he ever set foot in America, in the words of the judge, "You will go directly to jail. You will not pass Go, you will not collect two hundred dollars, and you will stay there for the next fifty years." Dr. Ivanov had never played Monopoly, so he didn't understand exactly what the judge meant, but he did leave on the next plane for his native Russia. He stayed there for the rest of his life and steered well clear of anything having to do with Vietnam, America, or pearls.

CHAPTER 29

THE PEARL OF GREAT PRICE

It was a week before they could leave Door County. The police and FBI had *lots* of questions for them, and the reporters had more. Also, it was several days before Mr. Nguyen, Dat, and Vladimir were well enough to travel.

Arthur and Kirstin liked Door County and the White Fish Inn had offered them free rooms for the week, but they were a little worried that their parents would insist that they come home immediately. But once Mr. and Mrs. Davis heard that General Tran and his men were all in jail, they told Arthur and Kirstin they could stay until everyone else was ready to leave. "Door County is a fun place, go explore it," Mr. Davis encouraged them. So they did.

Diem stayed with her father on his island. It was peaceful there, surrounded by trees and water. There was a little path to walk on and several big stones by the water that were perfect for sitting on and watching the sun come up or go down. Diem and her father had lots to talk about, of course, but Diem found that she also had lots to think about, and she spent hours and hours sitting on the rocks or walking slowly along the path.

After the security guards and Mr. Nguyen were discharged from the hospital, everybody drove back to Illinois. Diem, Mr.

Nguyen, Dat, and Vladimir continued on to Vietnam the next day after saying their good-byes to Arthur, Kirstin, and Officer MacGregor.

The night before his daughter left for Vietnam, Mr. LeGrand did not sleep. He spent the dark, quiet hours praying and wandering through the dewy grass of his fields as the horses slept and the crickets sang. He was wrestling with a momentous decision—Should he give the pearl to Diem or not? He was not at all sure that she was ready for it, but keeping it from her might not help. If he did not give it to her, the desire for it would gnaw at her heart. She might simply tell him whatever he wanted to hear in order to get it from him, and then act out a pretended faith whenever she was with him. That would be much worse than her present honest doubt. On the other hand, if he gave it to her, its beauty might distract her from the true Beauty she should be seeking, and possessing it might give her a jealous and selfish heart.

When he said good-bye to his daughter at the airport, he handed her a small box and said, "I don't want this to ever come between us, and I hope it never comes between you and God. What you do with it is now entirely up to you."

She opened the box and saw the Autumn Rose nestled inside. She gasped in joyful surprise. "I can't believe it! Oh, thank you, Papa!" She hugged him for the first time in over twenty-five years and then ran to catch her plane.

Two months later, Kirstin was at Mr. LeGrand's house riding Shadowfax, the Arabian gray she had admired when she first met "Jean-Luc St. Vincent." There was just the slightest nip in the air, and some of the leaves were beginning to turn yellow and red. She and Arthur were back in school, and they were both busy with sports and after-school activities, including a new case for the Davis Detective Agency. But they still came out to visit Mr. LeGrand as often as they could, usually on Saturday mornings, but not too early for Arthur's sake. They would have breakfast, followed by a morning ride for Kirstin and a lazy glass of lemonade in the morning sun for Arthur and Mr. LeGrand.

Kirstin rode Shadowfax around the field and then back toward the house with the idea of taking him to practice jumping on a small course that Mr. LeGrand had set up behind his home. As she rode by, however, she saw Arthur and Mr. LeGrand standing on the porch and waving to her. She rode over and dismounted. "What is it?" she asked.

"Here, read this," said Mr. LeGrand with a smile on his face. "I just got it from Diem. She didn't want me to tell anyone until the sale was final." He handed her a faxed newspaper article. It read, "NEW YORK—The Metropolitan Museum announced today that it has purchased an extremely large black pearl named the Autumn Rose. The pearl will be displayed in the Museum's gemology section. A special window will be built so that sunlight can fall on the pearl for as much of the day as possible, due to a remarkable radiance that the pearl acquires when exposed to the sun.

"The Museum did not disclose the purchase price, which anonymous sources have said was quite high. The Museum did issue a written statement emphasizing that it had assurances that the entire purchase price would be donated to charity.

"The Autumn Rose's seller has chosen to remain anonymous. However, the seller did release a statement through the Museum repeating that all proceeds from the sale would be donated to charities. Specifically, the money will be used to fund missionaries and Christian schools in Vietnam and China. The seller further stated that the pearl was being sold because the seller had 'recently acquired a pearl of infinitely greater price' than the Autumn Rose and felt that the Autumn Rose should now belong to the public."

"That is *so* cool," said Kirstin when she finished the article. "You must be so happy!" she said to Mr. LeGrand. "It's like . . . like . . ."

"Like the perfect ending to the case of the Autumn Rose?" suggested Arthur.

"Yeah," said Kirstin.

THE LOST TREASURE OF
FERNANDO MONTOYA

RICK ACKER

Don't miss the next nail-biting Davis Detective Mystery

The Lost Treasure of Fernando Montoya

0-8254-2005-9

Who knew that a 150-year-old mystery could be so dangerous? While Arthur and Kirstin Davis are visiting their uncle in San Francisco, a chance conversation at a baseball game puts them on the trail of 400 pounds of gold (yes, four *hundred* pounds) that vanished during the Gold Rush of 1849. But the teen detectives soon discover that someone wants them off the case.

The investigation quickly becomes a harrowing adventure exploring the treacherous old gold fields, scuba diving in the shark-infested waters of the San Francisco Bay, and managing to get inside one of the buried ships. But things *really* get dangerous when they finally uncover the secret of the lost treasure of Fernando Montoya.

Coming Spring 2003